THE RACHEL CONDITION

THE
RACHEL
CONDITION

Nicholas Rombes

FICTION

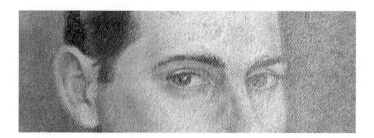

"Evie has a perverse desire to turn around and ride Red right straight for the man following her, and to have it be done with once and for all. To break with the script. To think thoughts and to say words she was never meant to say."

—*Beyond Blue Tomorrows*

I'VE ASSEMBLED THIS IN THE TRUEST WAY I KNOW HOW.
By memory, since nothing else is trustworthy. My letters
to Antony are preserved as they were recovered, mildly
redacted as I'd expected. Charlotte's report—her justifica-
tion—is here in full, although the weirdly formal and stilted
language will only feed into rumors that it's not authentic.
As evil as it is, I've kept the Colonel's letter to Antony as it
contains the revelation. The Colonel, Antony's father, his
eyes, my God!

What can I say here about Psycho Femmes that Antony
hasn't already said?

His account (fucked up, but still) of Detroit and what happened there—prompted by an analyst who told him to "tell it
like a story"—is also here in full. These have been arranged
in roughly the order he wrote them, ending with the account
of his imprisonment. Perhaps, after all, telling is not the same
as healing, as Antony's verbal disintegration as he reaches
the ground zero of his telling makes painfully clear. Beyond
that I can only say that all autobiography relies as much on
what's not said as what is. At the heart of his story is absence

and I've refrained mightily from filling in the gaps and from correcting his misperceptions. The instances where I've given into temptation and inserted my own version are hardly worth mentioning, although to the sensitive reader I'm sure they're obvious. Encouraged as he was to write about what happened in Detroit in a way that made him feel safe and at a slight remove from the events—in other words, to tell it like a story— it's clear where he succeeded and where he failed. I've placed most of the conversations he remembered into dialog form and corrected his numerous spelling errors.

Beyond Blue Tomorrows—the annotated version—is included here.

As for the arrangement of the texts, it is, after all, my story to tell.

As a rough guide to chronology:

Original publication of *Beyond Blue Tomorrows*: 1978
Psycho Femmes band: 1981
Charlotte's report: 1998
Antony in Detroit: 1999
The Colonel's letter to Antony: 1999
Antony's imprisonment: 1999–2003
My letters to Antony during his imprisonment: 1999–2002
Antony's version: 2005

Dedicated to my brother.

—Rachel, Detroit

March 24, 1999

Dear Antony,

Are you seeing two of everything?

I swore I wouldn't write to you, but here I am writing to you. Prison is hell, I know. I guess I can't really say that we're both prisoners—I won't insult you by saying that—but we are both bound and caged. My cage is larger than yours and it has no metal bars to speak of. Outside my window I can even see Fletcher's. I still call it that, even though what you and I knew as Fletcher's is gone, of course. I'm looking at it now: it looks the same from the outside, although the big red sign is gone. The street feels much like it did then—the trees are bigger, those that survived the ███ ten years ago. You were never to be ooo.

Never never never.

Are you receiving these letters? I can only hope so and I'm writing them to you so fully and unrestrained because that's the only way I know how.

There is something very important I want to tell you but I can't yet, not until I know for sure. In the months since you were taken so much has changed.

There's all the things you didn't know, you couldn't know, the little details and hints and, in your absence, I feel like I have to tell you. Maybe it's guilt, or remorse, or maybe it's just because I'm free without you, free to say things with no prospect of your response because you can't respond, can you?

I hope you don't blame me for what happened, although I'd understand if you did, even though I don't blame myself. After all it was YOU, Antony, who came to us and deceived us, and you must have known that you were walking into a very carefully laid trap. I don't want to get ahead of myself but there it is. God no I'm not writing to ask forgiveness although I've heard about some of what they've done to you and of course it makes me sick to think about. You were right that our side is as inventive as yours when it comes to hurting people.

Not that I've been treated well, but my punishment's been more indirect—I haven't lost any fingers or toes or eyes for what I did, or had plyers work on the back of my throat. And Julia . . . well, I'll come to that later. It's easy to look back and see all the mistakes we made, but I'm still not sure what I'd change. I couldn't change you coming, that's for sure. In fact (and no, I'm not going to go off on one of my free will digressions, do you remember those?!) don't think there's really much that I could have done differently, even if I'd wanted to. So much of what happened to us, Antony, all of us, was determined by forces so much larger than us. I couldn't undo that any more than I could undo history.

I can't tell you what I have to tell you, yet.

A pigeon has just landed on the windowsill where a thin layer of sand has collected. The window is open today and there's a warm breeze.

I smell honeysuckle.

There is the clatter of dishes somewhere in the distance. The ripeness of garlic.

The whine of a drone high in the sky.

You only notice the drones now when you don't hear them. In their absence.

The pigeon keeps looking my way and then away, its little purple oily head with its tiny little brain inside. Like I said, my room's near Fletcher's, on the ■■■ floor of a post-Warbrick building, right on the edge of a wasteland

and it's occupied by people mostly like me who I guess are undesirables, of a sort, because their loyalties are unsure or suspect. More and more of us fit into that category these days. I work across the street at a coffee shop and also sometimes fill in at the daycare center, the one with the bright yellow daisy as its symbol. I can't remember if that was here when you were here. When I moved in, the previous occupant had left a wind chime hanging on the little balcony and it drove me crazy at first but I didn't get around to taking it down and now the chime's grown on me, its pale little gentle sounds.

I want to remember things the way they really happened, not the way I remember remembering them. Paul once told me the reason he drank to blackout every few nights was to forget the terrible things he was doing. But I think he still remembered anyway. At least enough to talk about the techniques he used on bodies.

God I hope there are no Pauls where you are.

There's so much I want to tell you Antony, not only about what happened but what I fear is going to happen. I've been assured by someone there that you'll receive these letters, unopened and uncensored, but that they ▪▪▪ you write back. (Or are you physically unable to write back?) But how can I be sure? Like I said, I'm writing these as if you are receiving and able to read them, all doubt be damned. I want you to understand, I so badly want you to understand, WHY I did the things I did. I'm not going to apologize for them, no not ever, because what good would that do? I don't need your forgiveness, Antony. I don't know what I need. . .

Rachel

April 10, 1999

Antony,

The sun came out today, the first time in a long time. It felt so good on my face and arms. I wonder: is there sun where you are? My friend there will only tell me that they keep you underground, but I don't know if that means all the time.

Literally underground?

Do they take you out to see the light, to feel the air?

I know you can't answer me but I wonder. I wrote in the last letter that I was in a prison too, of a different sort, though yes I know prison is too strong a word.

I can leave my apartment when I want, I can walk the streets, I can listen to the radio, I can get a coffee, I can mail you these letters.

I have to be more careful now. I sometimes get tired. I have to rest more often. But Antony, I can feel the edges of my confinement.

I mentioned the wasteland earlier but that's just the informal name we've given it, this city-sized space we inhabit that feels like it's bounded, bounded by something unfamiliar. There are checkpoints, that much I know. And if you have the right ███, it's easy to come and go. The question is, what are the right ███? No one seems to know. But there's always some new story circulating about how so-and-so presented the correct blank and was free to leave.

I can picture you reading this right now, Antony, sitting on a cot with your knees up and your back against the wall. Even if it's a fantasy I HAVE to believe it or what's the point?

It's strange that even though I hope you're receiving my letters I really have no idea whether you even want them, let alone what you think about them. Why am I writing, then? Partly to let you know what's happening out here, and partly to revisit what we both learned just before they took you away: that we ███. Of course, we have no way to be absolutely sure, right? I wish you could correct me if I'm wrong, but since you can't, my understanding is that "The Colonel," wrote to you before.

It killed a part of me inside to learn that, to learn that about us. But then the other thing happened and I changed my thinking; I had to if I wanted to survive.

So many questions.

God are you even reading this?

The only way I can go forward is to assume it's true: why would ███ lie to you at the very end? And the timing is right too, in terms of where the Colonel was and when (I've done some research) ███ ███, and even certain ███ characteristics. So yes: I AM prepared to believe ███, Antony. It's the only way I can make sense of a life that up to now—to be honest—has felt scattershot and undirected. Does that even mean anything? It's as if—and I know how strange this sounds—it's as if I've always been waiting for that missing piece, even though I haven't known just what that piece is. Like I've been in idle, revving up all my life, just waiting for that right moment to drop into gear and go.

Do you remember when I touched you that first time?

May 20, 1999

Antony,

I'm sorry it's been so long, so much has happened here.

I don't know where to begin, or even if I should tell you about it at all. I felt them moving in me last night, really moving.

If I say it all in just one letter it'll sound even more absurd than it is, so I'll just tell you, for now, about what happened at the coffee shop. You don't know it because it wasn't finished when you were here; it opened right after you left ("you left!"—of course you didn't leave, you were taken away; I promise I'll try to write honestly about what happened to you—to us—and not coat it with sugary words) . . . Anyway, the coffee shop—it's called—it's across the street and about a block away from Fletcher's and it's where I go, very often, to write these letters. The shop is tiled in pale, sea-foam green that reminds me of a restroom. Maybe it was intended to evoke something like Art Deco or even maybe the Fifties, I don't know. But it feels like a huge restroom and then of course scouring that from your mind while you're drinking the coffee. . .

But for some reason, it's one of the only places where it feels safe to post what we used to call "political" flyers. There's a small corkboard behind the cream and sugar station where people have tacked up quotes, sayings, sometimes even mimeographed pamphlets like in the old days. My guess for why they allow it—and the reason I've not yet contributed anything—is because they watch to see who tacks stuff up. I've no evidence whatsoever, and in fact some of the people I've seen putting up even the most provocative political work keep showing up here week after week. Obviously, no one is "taking them away." Some of the slogans seem deliberately wrong, like they've been cut and pasted from another time, like SMASH THE CAPITALIST ROADERS or YOU MUST BURN THE OLD GRASS FOR THE NEW TO GROW.

And yet, I'm cautious, Antony. YOU of all people must understand why. But the corkboard isn't why I'm telling you this—I just wanted you to know what sort of place it is, a sort of place that seems a bit freer, a bit more open than others. That's why it seemed so strange to me that I should react so strongly—and so irrationally—to a young man sitting across the room from me, drinking a coffee (of course!) working on his screen, ear buds in. He was wearing a black turtleneck, and he wasn't looking at me.

THAT'S the point. I can usually tell when a person is trying NOT to look at me. But it was more than that, it was the fact that there was nothing on his screen. I know because the restrooms were behind him and when I came out I saw: he was fake-typing. He caught me in the reflection on his screen, paused for a second, and then continued typing. I went back to my table across the room, but by the time I got there and glanced over his way, he was gone.

I'll admit I'm more sensitive than most when it comes to being watched. It happened again a few days later. The same guy, doing the same thing, making even more of a show of NOT looking at me. Everything's changed so fast since you were here. It's hard to tell the difference between the Pauls and Julias of us and the others, the more radical ones among us, like the ones who took you. Do you see what I mean about nothing being as free as it seems? Compared to you, of course not, I know, and yet I too feel caged, and the guy with the laptop is the least of it. There's so much that's happened—so many small incidents and events that seem to be warning me to leave. I've started keeping track of them and maybe if something happens to me (happens, there's a juicy euphemism for you) these letters (assuming you're keeping them) will shed some small light on the whole rotten system, of which you and I are a part, like ■■■■ before us. The first thing I want to tell you about is the phones, and who might be listening on the phones.

You don't know how what we started ended, what it led to. Not yet. I have to tell you.

But not right now.

There's probably no way you would know this, but we've regressed back to old fashioned, rotary phones. I still sometimes find myself automatically about to "push" the numbers rather make that finger-in-circle-then-make-a-circle motion, a motion which I've come to find oddly soothing and an activity that requires patience, and even contemplation. I don't use the phone that much—the people I need to talk with I can talk with in person, most of the time. But sometimes I do need to call, and when I do, it's as if there's a third presence, on the line, hovering there in the silence between words, in the low hum of the electrical current. Do you know that feeling you sometimes get that you're being watched, that someone's eyes are on you? It's a different sort of feeling than how the drones make you feel. Maybe because we know they're watching. But whether they are or not, what difference does it make? That's the point isn't it? We've internalized the feeling of being watched. No, this other feeling, it's unscientific, I'm sure, but it feels real. That's how the listener on the phone is; it's as if that anonymous ear pressed against the receiver creates a vacuum, a vacuum that suggests presence, not absence. Not like the drones. You've felt that absence before, haven't you Antony? When we were together, before we knew . . .

June 9, 1999

Antony,

Here's a terrible thought experiment: it didn't matter, any of it. Your side, my side.

The "protectorate." The "insurgents." The "rezidentis."

All the other stupid, inadequate names we called others and we were called. The outcome was predetermined.

Our differences were measured in gradations smaller than grains of sand. Raw power shing from one side of a barrel to another.

Do you remember how you lit that first cigarette for me at Fletcher's? I watched your face very slyly and very carefully as I leaned in. You have beautiful eyelashes, did you know? Long and black and feminine. In all honesty that's one of the things that attracted me to you. Your hand trembled. That sweet mole on your knuckle that seemed so uncannily familiar. Did you know that, or that I wanted to lean in even further and kiss you? Or that my world trembled just a little bit when you were that close? And I could feel that I trembled yours?

You weren't the only one with ███ desires Antony, were you? Everything is different in retrospect.

Maybe I'm remembering those moments the way I wish they had unfolded rather than how they actually did, but so what if I am? It's my history and yours and it's ours alone(for now) to fuck up and rearrange. I can write it and write it and write it over and over again and the results always equal us kissing that first time. Wanting to so badly and then doing it. The shadow of Paul looming, the drones stitching through the night reminding us of all the things we built to kill us . . .

Antony please. Please come back.

Antony's Case Prepared by
(the Bitch) Charlotte Malums

ANTONY WAS MINE. AS IN, MY SELECTION.

I want to get this right. I want to be very clear. I'm not writing this for any other reason than to be right, and to be clear. Rightness and clarity. I don't care about ornament. I don't care about rhetoric. I was born to be a bureaucrat, what can I say.

If there's going to be a record (and what fuck all isn't there a record of these days?) let it show (let me show) that I made this decision against the counsel of others, and so take full responsibility. By the time Antony has either succeeded or failed my position here will no longer exist, and although that does not absolve me of my complicity in the outcome the question is, for me, merely existential. *Merely existential.* That's the sort of thing Antony would say, isn't it, though you wouldn't know it to hear others describe him. Let me guess: he'll come across in Detroit as a sentimental sort of guy, a bit of a romantic, a bit naïve but in a pleasing kind of way. Unless you—like me—find it all just a bit too much, considering the appalling things we know our Antony to be capable of, especially when it comes to his own family. Especially when it comes to betrayal. Especially when it comes to self- deception, which is just another form of betrayal. Especially when it comes to selective amnesia. Especially when it comes to denying himself the very things—the very people— who would bring him pleasure. Especially when it comes to his capacity to play the martyr, a part for which the Colonel trained him all too well. Let me guess: if Antony finds himself, at the end of the day, bound up in some dark cell with a pierced eardrum and the majority of the 27 bones in his right hand broken he'll brook no refusal to frame his predicament in the worst possible light. As if we aren't, each one of us, responsible for our own fate. If this testament is included in whatever almanac or record survives, then hope it will shed some light on *that* side of Antony, the side I'm familiar with, uncensored by him or his father. There we are with fathers again. The original fuckers, are they not? What of mothers, and their absence here? Pauls, but what of Paulines? Antonys, but what of Antonias?

What names did he go by back then? Oh yes, *Anthony*, when he wanted to fuck with people as a joke, although though the joke (as if the universe was eternally slanted against him) usually ended up on him. *Tony*? No, never. That one he positively hated.

Was Antony prepared for the revelation that awaited him in Detroit? Was Rachel?

To discover *that* person, only to discover something else, too?

Antony was prepared for that no more than he was *prepared to be born.*

We had all been versed in Marx's tired axiom: *The class which has the means of material production at its disposal has control at the same time over the means of mental production.* But only so that we could reverse it: *The class which has the means of mental production at its disposal has control at the same time over the means of material production.* We understood—as the insurgents did as well—that the era of material production was over: at stake was the production of mental images, of spectacle beyond even what Debord imagined, a constant flow not of things but of ideas represented as icons, images, logos, aphorisms. Nostalgic as the insurgents were for nature and the so-called *natural world*, our theorists wondered this: could we detour nature itself into a symbol, our symbol? What about sentiment or, better yet, love? Could we make it so that love itself was associated exclusively with the protectorate?

And here's where our Antony's sense of fellow feeling for the past comes into play, for who better to send on a mission like this than someone for whom the so-called natural world was the bottom line? The *real thing*, as Antony might say. For here's a man who—although he's read all the requisite deconstructive theory—still believes in stable ground. As in rocks, trees, the clay of the earth. As in a hard-core reality, none of that Baudrillard *simulacrum* bullshit. So of course he's suited for *Beyond Blue Tomorrows*. He's its ideal reader. The endless deserts in that book consumed, eventually, everyone who read it except, of course, for me. Bureaucrats always survive.

As a woman in this protectorate I've endured the harassment and platitudes not of men, but of women, and my decision to send Antony—rather than Caroline, Jazmin, or Selena—is one that gives me no uncertain pleasure. And yet all things considered, wasn't Antony the best *qualified* for the Detroit excursion, given his past trauma and his delicate, unstable relationship with his own personal history? His penchant for melodrama? His feigned empathy for those he is about to hurt? His willed lack of awareness, his dangerous innocence, when it comes to the suffering of others? As you can plainly see, the question should not be, *How could I send Antony?* but rather, *How could I send anyone BUT Antony?*

Let's just cut through the bullshit: Antony usually greeted me with a hard-on.

I respected it, that hard-on, but was never curious enough to do anything with it.

While others flinched at what we did to the living bodies in the basement, Antony watched, not without a certain remorse for the witnessing of it. Other supposedly stronger candidates could learn much from observing and reflecting upon our Antony's ability to witness and, albeit in a detached way, feel the suffering of others while understanding the importance—the necessity—of this suffering for the health of the political project we've set before us.

Detroit: a place of suffering, calloused and yet open to the shaky, empathic vision that Antony will bring, Antony who still called me Commander despite my invitations to call me Charlotte, and who sat across from my desk so many times with an uncertain, rigid (if you get my drift) formality despite my gestures toward an off-the-record relationship. On more than one occasion I've caught him looking at the faded Borromean rings tapestry that hangs behind my desk, hiding a small hole in the cinderblock wall that separates my office from the black room which adjoins it. And on other occasions he seems to have noticed the mirror *behind* the mirror in my office. And yet on other occasions I've watched Antony as he watched me and observed not only an awareness, on his part, of this double-looking but also a remarkable *adaptability* to my shifting signals. These natural skills (if he honors them) should do him well in Detroit and in the undefined, fluid political environment that has made that city such a vexed burden for so long. A city that's resisted the simple protections we've offered.

Having said this, I want my report to be as unambiguous and pure and reflective of the same shaped reality as the protectorate's own ideology. By which I mean: Antony's mission to Detroit conforms to a vision of our future that will come to pass because we are *imagining* that future into existence through an ironclad set of principles threaded through all our actions, with the rare exception of those very few places, such as Detroit, where the purity of our signal is degraded and where we require someone like Antony to be present ("on the ground," as they used to say) and alert to the sorts of subtle, gestural moments that are, if not undetectable, then at the very least undecipherable from a physical distance. And Antony, based on my years-long experience as his Charlotte (despite the fact that he insists on calling me "Commander") responds viscerally and openly and without pretense to my *comings-on*, making him, I believe, receptive to the woman he will meet and befriend in Detroit. There is no pretense like the pretense of attraction, a lesson which I myself have experienced and tried to instill here at the compound, from the highest echelons right on down to the tortured prisoners, prisoners for whom the shiny instruments of torture become, at the very end, fragile and tender appendages of the family itself.

The truth is we were never fully confident in our power and that's what led us to keep probing at the edges, in places like Detroit. And to offer the lure of protection. If we had just trusted ourselves, trusted that even if places like Detroit and Cincinnati and Buffalo and Toledo did breed disruptors, it wouldn't have amounted to anything coherent or strategic enough to count as serious threats.

Don't fuck with fuckers or **Don't fuck with fuckers or you'll get fucked** is what our motto should have been.

But because who we were was forged in theory, in abstractions, we were never settled enough to trust ourselves because if there's one thing theory teaches you it's that everything—even theory itself—is untrustworthy. We didn't trust ourselves, let alone our theories, and what regime can succeed with weak thoughts like that? Like a patient who keeps poking at her wounds to make sure they're healing, only to slow them from healing, we kept sending out instigators like Antony, who himself needed healing and was in no condition to go anywhere, least of all Detroit. I'm sure he'll encounter what's left of the band Psycho Femmes and their sick counterparts Yama.

So yes, Antony's susceptibility to the sways of desire, of feeling, of affect—echoed by the structures of the protectorate itself—figured heavily into my decision, and if this sentimental tendency in Antony is something I've overestimated, then of course I'll accept the consequences (as if I have any choice in the matter.) For I've come to know Antony not only as an agent of our cause, but also an agent of his own, which makes him vulnerable to the sorts of seduction that likely awaits him in Detroit. Although I'm known as someone whose cool words rarely betray the sort of so-called inhumane actions I've taken to maintain what we have rightly earned, I will say that if, in selecting Antony, I have made a mistake that may result in the undoing of everything we have worked for, then I would like it to be known that it was the invisible hands of Caroline, Jazmin, and Selena that, inadvertently, helped me along in my decision. Their envy helped fuel my determination that MY choice must not be THEIR choice.

My doubts about Antony may seem trivial: will he wear the items he's been instructed to wear? The bracelet and, more importantly, the boots? The boots with the protective soles? For the record, I instructed him to wear the boots, but not why to wear them. If this is because, at some level, I wanted him to fail then so be it. Why should the one who awaits him in Detroit have him? He's mine to have or to discard.

I have selected Antony. In our own way, we all have.

He is on his own now, to return to us whole, or in pieces.

Antony

THE PLANE CAME IN LOW AFTER BEGINNING ITS DESCENT over Chicago, sling-shotting beyond Detroit, banking hard left. Crossing over parts of Ontario and then Grosse Ile, in the Detroit River, before hitting the tarmac with a bump and a sudden twist and pop that suggested how easy it would be for everything to go terribly wrong.

Arrived in Detroit. Almost crashed.

But there are gaps in my story, in my memory of my story. They said that because of what happened to me there are gaps and there always will be. Did I know I was being monitored at the time? I'm sure I did. I must have. It was Charlotte, after all, who'd sent me. Did I know that the level of monitoring included recording some of my conversations? That I'd been bugged? Not really, although if you'd told me at the time I wouldn't have been surprised. More likely, I'd have been flattered. In the protectorate's eyes I was an information collection machine. That much I understood. The tapes helped me write this, but not as much as you'd think. Once I began it was all there as fresh as yesterday and I used the recordings mostly to try to capture the way they talked, Rachel and Julia especially, the patterns of their speech. Because that meant a lot to me and still in my memories

I'm more likely to recall one of Rachel's odd phrasings or inversions of words than what it was she actually said. So, listening back to her pauses, her laughs, the way she spoke my name, stressing the long o in Antony rather than the flatter Anteny—the texture and grain of her voice was more useful than any recordings ever could be in helping me remember the details of what happened. And, of course, there are conversations I'd misremembered or forgotten and I hope that setting them down here will help slow the rushing thoughts, the constant effort to remember.

The Colonel (I've been urged to refer to him as father but I'm not there yet) was one of the protectorate's theorists and I suppose I can't escape the way his mind worked, always looking for patterns, trying to impose some abstract meaning on a brief, chaotic moment of history. I'm told the surest way to rehabilitation is to focus on the small details of what happened in Detroit.

But I don't want to be some wounded storyteller.

I don't believe in the old structures of thought I've been told will help me: the quest narrative, the chaos narrative, the so-called restitution narrative. But writing, the analyst says, will help normalize my memories so that they seem naturally a part of who I am instead of some weird extension. A *second self*, my analyst calls it. (And which self does she present to me, I wonder?) Which is strange because the most insidious legacy of the protectorate was the mirror institutions they'd created, the so-called parallel structures which started small. In Detroit, the first parallel institution, I'd learned from Charlotte, were small businesses, like Big Red's Groceries on Fenkel, a mom-and-pop grocery store with the wilted, weathered, burlap awning that swiftly became more popular than the large supermarket across the battered street. Next, it was a few homegrown churches, some spelled Baptist and some Baptiste, which made all the difference. A put-together carwash from an old gas station on Puritan where they used something like old sleeping bags to dry off the cars. A bar with a red tin overhang at Midland and Hubbell called The Reason Why. A tire repair shop on Curtis with an enormous fiberglass replica of a Michelin tire, covered in bird shit, on a crooked pole. After these took hold it was on to bigger, bolder parallel organizations: a police station that offered more security than the official neighborhood precinct. A new school made of recovered cinder blocks on a cluster of abandoned, narrow lots on Six Mile. As the protectorate systematically undermined the original organizations, they had prepared for alternative, parallel ones.

Even a fancy name like *metastrategic knowledge* couldn't obscure what we all knew about the drones: that they had developed the ability not just to adapt, but to *think* about adapting. To be aware, and to be aware of awareness. But wasn't this a relief, after all? We'd finally freed ourselves from having to think *for* them. To be freed from an entire line of thinking and all the boring evolutionary twists that would come. Better to leave that to the drones themselves, because how much thought can a person take, how heavy the burden to not just think for ourselves and for others but also for the stupid machine-heads inside those drone cockpits? Let the drones think for themselves, was what I said, and call it whatever you want.

I came to Detroit for a simple reason: to embed myself within a cell of persistent radicals among the rezidentis, as they say, and to report my findings back to the Commander. (She insisted on that absurd title. "The Commander," Charlotte, whose cement-walled, torture chamber-like office suggested the terror of a purely administrative mind and whose directive to me was delivered *in person* and with the seductive familiarity of some ancient ritual, as if sliding a pale envelope across the polished surface of a steel desk was a gesture akin to enacting the Eucharist.)

But how?

By what means?

My cover story was simple and direct: to track down the annotated, pre-publication manuscript version of *Beyond Blue Tomorrows*. The novella had been published at the height of the conflict, before everything splintered and sub-groups of sub-groups flowered and withered and re-constituted themselves in what felt like cycles that had no center. Both sides were devolving into smaller and smaller cells, the protectorate experimenting with normalizing outrageous violence that would have been unthinkable just a few years earlier, and the insurgents (I prefer the term radicals but apparently that's fallen out of favor) following various theory-inspired event-scenes that suggested they had either lost their way or were onto something really powerful. *Tomorrows* had been published during that time and quickly became a kind of blank slate for both sides to interpret as a vindication of their own beliefs, something like a parable that shifted meanings depending on what parts you emphasized. Charlotte and others had become obsessed with claiming it as an allegory (that's what she called it) whose main characters' adventures were symbolic of the protectorate's heroic quest for order.

When it first appeared—by an unknown press in a ratty paperback format that looked old and used right from the start—I'd read it as a short, weird adventure story, something like a super-compressed *Huck Finn* except set in a desert with a woman on a horse rather than in a river with a boy on a raft. My copy's worn cover featured a dark red sun, like a soft, melted marble in the sky, hanging low over a desert with a tiny black figure in the distance that you couldn't even tell if it was human or not. I'd spent a lot of time in my small bedroom with the worn-down blue shag above the Colonel's office staring at that cover (I thought of it as a painting) searching for something, even now I'm not sure what. I remember the cover feeling lurid, something like a dangerous zone that you had to enter very carefully, and being unsure whether or not the figure following the woman on the horse was even human. There was a crease in my copy that obscured the figure even more and I remember the feeling of how time passed slower during my absorption in the painting.

I'd loved the story's strange familiarity, as if the remote, vast, unfamiliar desert setting contained enough space for me to imagine myself in the story itself. And I suppose that's why both sides took it as their own, re-did the covers to reflect the ideas they saw at the heart of the book, used it as a rallying point for their own ideologies. Who were those anonymous artists who remade the cover for each new paperback printing, on cheaper and cheaper paper it seemed, as many as ten or so different editions a year at the peak of the book's popularity? *Beyond Blue Tomorrows* endorsed x ideas and rejected y ideas. Or else the other way around. Evie—the protagonist—was either a hero or a villain, a restorer of order or an insurgent bent on destroying order. She was either one of us or them. Or, in crossing borders on her horse, she was both us and them. Readers were supposed to follow her story in hopes she would be victorious, or in hopes that she would fail.

We collected and traded the little books and I'd spend time on my bedroom floor—how old was I, nine or ten?—sorting them by sides. It seemed like the protectorate's covers focused on the heroic dimensions of the desert structure—an enormous stone well—that Evie was sent to sabotage, while the insurgent covers actually depicted Evie herself in a way that, while not too much like propaganda, really showed her as some sort of hero figure. By the 50th or 60th printing it had become a cliché to depict Evie on her horse, silhouetted against an enormous burnt-orange sun. Sometimes she was slumped forward, drenched, in a kind of martyred exhaustion, her broad shoulders still strong while at other times she was sitting erect in the saddle, not a drop of sweat on her, her hands firmly on the reins and her gaze set straight ahead fixed on her distant goal.

I figured those were insurgent printings, while the ones foregrounding the structure were the protectorate's. In some of those covers Evie wasn't even there at all. Just the well, its vast red rim encircling pure black nothingness. I liked those covers, too, especially the one that somehow suggested movement *inside* the well, a smudge of black ink down in the center of the well, a circle blacker still than the blackness that surrounded it and, if I was lucky, surrounded me. Did I really believe the smudge moved just slightly when I held the book at a certain angle, in a certain light? I remember that I believed it, but did I? It doesn't matter because now I remember it as moving.

During that era the Colonel would sometimes encourage me to read passages aloud to him while he puttered in the garden, something I only realized later he did after committing some atrocious act in the basement. *Page 49*, he'd bark, *read the bottom of page 49*, and so I would, the bitter smell of black upturned earth rising up. Crouched down before me, working without gloves in soil, he'd sometimes mouth the words silently as I read, as if hearing me say them confirmed them, made them real. Even monsters appear vulnerable in certain slants of light and I remember staring at the back of the Colonel's thick, sweaty neck there in the garden, and the way one of his ears was misshapen in the form of something like a melted seashell. At those moments he seemed harmless and even vulnerable and I frightened myself at how easy it would be to take him at face value right then and there: nothing more than an ordinary man in an ordinary garden. I could pretend he wasn't the Colonel, that he was just a father, a father kneeling in a garden in the sun.

But that was so long ago. It wasn't until I was sent to Detroit that I began remembering him again.

*

Detroit. I was picked up at the dimly lit, abandoned-looking metro airport in Romulus after a ten-hour flight by an emissary of my motel, a man with extremely large hands and knuckles and yet the softest of voices, as he spoke to me about the city's peculiar history. He wore a black or navy-blue chauffeur's cap with a polished brim, I remember. His too-big hands smelled, I suspected, like mint. He drove like he was above the law, his frame filling the front seat, with a recklessness that approached something more like a parody of driving.

Had Charlotte sent him, or was I on my own now? I ditched the bracelet I'd been instructed to wear.

I kept the ugly black boots with the thick soles until I could find something more comfortable.

The chauffeur's eyes fixed on me in the rearview mirror as if in anticipation of my reaction but I played it cool, and didn't bother to fasten my seatbelt. For a sizeable amount of time while we were on the freeway he spoke as if we were travelling through the cramped dark back alleys and lost neighborhoods of the city, gesturing and grunting.

The dome light flickered, piss yellow, weakly whenever we hit a bump. We pulled over at a gas station, everything bathed in pink neon.

There was a bat, I remember, flitting about in an epileptic fit beneath one of the enormous purple overhangs. At first I thought it was a broken black umbrella caught in the wind but there was too much intention behind it. Inside the gas station, behind the greasy glass (blood-streaked, I thought) a hooded figure appeared to be swaying behind the counter. I got out to stretch while Lars (so read his name tag) went in to pay for the gas.

The night air was strong and grassy and I could imagine an enormous green swamp behind the gas station, the mist rising off it, deceiving in its beauty but deadly, the kind of place where bodies disappear. I could also imagine that around back of the gas station there was a metal door, a second door, an *unofficial* door not used by employees but reserved for someone special. In fact, upon the door was spray-painted, in choppy letters, THE ONE WHO COMES IN THE NIGHT. There was, as usual, the soft, high whining of drones, obscured by the night sky.

With the snap of the gas handle we were back in the car, which smelled like lemons, and soon beyond the freeways laid out like asphalted-over riverbeds. Detroit in its dark, underpowered magnificence loomed in the distance. Half-lit buildings and the hulking shadows of the unlit ones. Lars was very quiet, I remember that, and softer-eyed as if approaching a cathedral city. Soon we were at the small hotel across the street from the campus where I was summoned by the portly night attendant directly to my room (*don't bother, Lars will take care of your paperwork at the desk*) and then I was undressing and then I was on the soft bed. I noticed that on the open windowsill in the dark there sat an animal that could either have been a cat or raccoon or a fox and that its orange eyes were watching me. Charlotte had told me to be alert to small, unexpected moments like this because what she was after were the fine-grained details of life in this uncontrolled part of Detroit. I slept well in a bed with cold, over-chlorined white sheets but only after stuffing a thin blanket in the gap at the bottom of the bathroom door to stop the sound of the dripping water in the tub and the weird echo it made.

In the morning, the open city beckoned. The city that had been a legend in our minds, represented by charts and graphs and user manuals, a pocket of resistance that had emerged, my father said, because its purposefully broken infrastructure made it difficult for the protectorate to penetrate. Its inefficiency worked as a sort of shield, a barrier that protected it from the sorts of tools that relied on workable systems. Other cities, they worked, they were penetrable. Chicago, New York, St. Louis, Atlanta. That's why Charlotte insisted on sending me, I thought. As the Colonel's son, she supposed I was more able to tune into the subtle, low frequencies that the protectorate had missed through its heavy handed surveillance.

So, as instructed, I noticed.

The wires all pulled out of the tilted, gutted street lamps.

The abandoned and condemned houses tagged ooo in black spray paint, a code that would take me a while to understand.

The blown apart bus shuttle stops.

The old red street bricks glistening through the thin, pocked asphalt.

The slender, looming, repurposed antenna towers rising up like enormous insect feelers.

The trees that inexplicably had been painted white and the piles of dust in the boulevard islands.

The dated, rusted, over-sized, boxy surveillance cameras tenuously attached to splintered telephone poles.

The under-pixelated sign for a transmeter repair shop. The heaped, rusted garbage truck left in decay.

I followed my instincts into a place called Fletcher's. Charlotte hadn't told me the name, but I was sure this was it. The door was ajar. Heavy gray steel, propped open with a chipped cinder block. It was spring, after all. There was a long wooden bar to my left, a black banner with the usual abstract symbols hanging over it, a very tall bartender in the shadows with a bruised eye or an eye-patch, and some tables. Only now can I say that gravity felt a little different there, a little weaker and you could feel this immediately and see it in the way the cigarette smoke curled up high near the tin ceiling, smoke from a single cigarette in an ashtray at an empty table at the back.

I took a seat at the bar and waited as the bartender, his back to me, polished a glass.

It seemed his back was always to me at first. The place was disguised cleverly, but with subtle errors that suggested a deeper understanding of how people like me ferreted out places like this. The cult flag, for instance, above the bar, indicated an affinity for one of the protectorate's unofficial radical working groups whose unsanctioned methods were broadcast, on occasion, on graphic broadsides.

And yet the flag's silver emblems were slightly under proportioned. I remember that so well.

A swipe at the protectorate which I suppose someone must have thought only insiders would get. But Charlotte had trained me how to be an insider.

A perfect flag was as much of a tell as an imperfect flag, and it was my job to read such signals correctly, to parse through the fine lines of careful miscommunication. When the giant bartender finally turned to me I'd already learned something: that he hadn't yet formed a judgment about me. He shuffled more than walked, which made him seem less dangerous, which I suppose was the point. His broad face was damaged as many faces had been damaged years ago, burned and then healed in that way that suggested damp wax paper.

"Mitchum's a bum, am I right?" he said, arms folded. I'd been prepared for this.

"He can't hit for hitting," I said, "that's for sure."

"But then again he's better than Sinclair."

"I'm not so sure. Sinclair had an eye."

"For girls."

We laughed, or at least I laughed, and I understood that my time here would not be easy. He served me one drink, then two. The room took on a dull orange glow from the setting sun. The feeling of crawling through an oil painting. I remember that. And also the cup. A warm breeze blew some leaves and a red plastic cup in through the propped open door. The cigarette on the far back table had long ago burned itself out. The bartender polished glasses, and then disappeared, and then returned to polish more glasses. A distant phone rang.

I thought of Charlotte, too, and her short, cropped, licorice black hair and what she had promised me if my assignment in Detroit proved successful.

And what I had promised her.

What *had* I promised her?

*

The door swung open and she (I would soon learn her name was Rachel) stepped in, paused, and walked straight to the table in back with the dead cigarette. She looked familiar but not like someone from real life, rather from a painting or a photograph, or a memory of a painting or photograph. She wore a blue or purple beret. A black sweater which seemed uncalled for in this weather. She took a seat at the bar, removed her beret (it was neither blue nor purple, but rather black) and sighed. Her hair was cut sharply across her forehead in the style of the previous decade and suddenly I understood that, just as I had not wandered in here by accident, neither had she. She placed a small notebook between us covered in what brought to mind the skin of an alligator, green and glinty.

Something fell out of her hair, like sand.

She fingered the ice in her drink and then began to talk in a familiar way, as if picking up the thread of a previous conversation even though I'd just met her for the first time today. She asked what brought me to Detroit and I remember feeling relieved, somehow, that she had come right out with the question. It gave me a chance, of course, to tell her about *Beyond Blue Tomorrows* but more than that, for at the moment of telling her I realized that in my lie there was a truth, because what had *brought me to Detroit* was to watch, to learn, to collect information which I'd divulge to Charlotte upon my return but also, yes, to lay hands on, if possible, the annotated version (if such a thing existed) of *Tomorrows*.

Rachel mentioned that the old Detroit University used to house forgotten manuscripts but that during the protectorate's short-lived incursion into the city, the university had served as one of the metropolitan detention centers. She said that the sandstone clock tower was once used for surveillance, and then later as a broadcast tower for the terrible wave signals, and that this entire city quadrant had been under its gaze, under its sonic assault. *I don't know if I should be telling you this,* she said, *but one drink in . . .* and then went on to describe the body cages beneath the library in great detail, and by the time the bartender returned, wiping the palms of his hands down the front of his shirt, it was clear to me that she had spent time there, in those cages.

The fountain in the center of campus, she said, was where they'd drowned her friend holding her head beneath the water with a tine bow rake to the back of her neck. The bartender was now once more behind the bar with something like a cracked smile across his lips. Without being asked he prepared another drink for Rachel, who had taken off an earring and placed it in her empty glass. (It was only much later, near the end of it all, that I would come to understand that this was how she paid for her drinks, a form of bartering that characterized all her actions.)

"You'll die from that," she said.

"From what?"

"Drinking. Right, Paul?"

Paul, I'd just learned, was the bartender. Paul.

Paul, who is also called Saul.

Sometimes Rachel called him Pauline and I came to understand that Paul/Pauline was an uncertain name and that at an earlier time Paul had been, they say, Pauline. But maybe in name only. Had Pauline changed, or just her name?

"God, this place," Rachel said, trying (or so I thought at the time) to get Paul's attention. She was wearing red sunglasses.

It's details like that I remember the most.

In fact I remember everything about Rachel the most.

Her large hands.

Her soft bulk.

The way she held your eyes in conversation as if she was waiting to tell you the most important thing in the world. She began telling me this long story about a recent betrayal, a close friend to whom she had loaned a large sum of money and who had subsequently disappeared, *like that!*—she snapped her fingers in front of her face—as if to emphasize the poof of disappearance, and before I could say anything she said *I'm not asking for money and I'm not asking for anything, I just want to talk,* as if she hadn't already established that earlier and I wanted to say, *Hey, I've got my own problems too you know, you're not the only one,* but of course who says things like that in real life? Thinking back on it now and re- listening to the tapes, it strikes me that it was just like Rachel to start like that, telling a story about people who were complete strangers to me. Even now I'm not sure how much of it was nothing more than what it seemed and how much of it was designed.

That bitch, Karen, Rachel said suddenly, signaling with a nod of the head to the deformed Paul-waiter for another round, summoning him in such a way that I can only describe as secret code-ish, and what I mean by that is that she gently flicked her earlobe and nodded and glanced his way . . . and this was not the first nor the last gesture which made me wonder whether they had known each other for a very long time and if the joke, ultimately, was on me. That *bitch Karen*, it turned out, had been so close a friend that Rachel considered her a sister. She was a kleptomaniac nymphomaniac (in so many words) who slept with a bank manager in exchange for certain codes and passwords that resulted in the emptying of Rachel's bank account, an account that had just recently been filled with an enormous sum from her father's trust.

Like I knew Detroit, I knew the insurgents, which is to say that I didn't understand either of them. I knew facts: names, dates, events, the seismic dot-points on Detroit's rise and fall and rise, the ostensible names of the key dissidents, the event-scenes of their strategic triumphs in the years leading up to the protectorate's fall, and then the sudden reversals that brought the protectorate back in a wash of blood and guts. How *Beyond Blue Tomorrows* kept switching back and forth—depending on how you read it—as a pro- insurgent novel or an anti-insurgent one.

And yet these details existed within the realm of facts, and facts were no longer a commodity. Once poisoned with doubt, facts became shadowy things drained of authority and meaning and import and so people like me were sent to go beneath the vast, oily surface of the truth, to go deep down into the cool clear realm of feeling. The Colonel had, at least, taught me that.

It was a new strategy I was using, *affect mining*, though none of us called it that. We still used the old romantic terms: detection, mission, assignment.

But *affect mining*—despite the lack of ring to it—captures best what people like me did: entering the insurgent areas and feeling around for, well, *feeling*. Affect. Keeping our antennae up for those subtle waves of feeling, of lust, ambition, hurt, fear, anxiety, ferreting them out with something like a sixth sense, a slight fluttering behind the ear. Like a thin, nearly invisible fishing line that leads not so much down but across vast geographic spaces bringing me here, finally, to Detroit, to this place called Fletcher's.

And I knew something else.

That sooner or later the very information I had come here to gather would be revealed, because that's how things happened between the agents of the protectorate and the agents of the insurgency back then, a sort of open-secret exchange of information, as if it wasn't information itself that was the valuable commodity, but rather life itself. If that sounds too abstract let me put it this way: the reason no one volunteered for these missions was because they were, in essence, suicide missions. As I was sitting there with Rachel I couldn't help but wonder if I'd already been had, if I'd already been discovered and if it was just a matter of time before I was disappeared, like those others of the protectorate who had come before me.

Because what was being traded were lives, not information.

It was a curious, even deformed mechanism for maintaining the sort of low-level, churning violence necessary to keep both sides in a perpetual, slow civil war, and although I only understood imperfectly what my role in the whole absurd process was, I did know enough to recognize and understand that I was, probably, doomed.

*

"Have you been to the greenhouse yet?" Rachel asked. I didn't understand.

"Which one?"

She smiled. "Hear that Pauli," she said, not taking her eyes off me, "he doesn't know 'which' greenhouse."

Paul shrugged.

"Well, thank God there's only one. The protectorate's first station in Detroit. They built it during their second, longer settlement here, supposedly with enslaved insurgents but I don't believe that part. It's funny when you think about it. Brilliant, really. How much they hated the natural world because they hadn't made it and yet how much they relied on it for their methods."

"Hadn't made it, as in?"

'Nature has no ideology' and all that. Remaking nature was a part of their power and yet there they were replicating it in the greenhouse. Of course, that's not all they were replicating, but you know that," she said, holding my eyes. What did I see when I looked into them then, her green eyes, what did I really see? Behind the little flecks of brown (like sand) around her pupils? And the pupils themselves like small drops of discolored mercury.

"So who sent you here?"

"No one," I said. Then I told her the rest, Charlotte's script, almost word for word: the concocted story about how I'd been a linguistics professor in California and, as chair, had protected my faculty the best I could. About how my department was the last holdout, the last to sign the New Standards document, the last to resist. How when it came time to give them a list of *those* faculty I gave them a piece of paper with only one name on it: mine. How I'd been permitted to carry out my research as an independent scholar.

"So you were complicit," Rachel said, as if it was a fact. "I wasn't. I was independent."

"You use that word like a shield. As if it'll protect you."

"From?"

"My judgment."

"I never did anything to help the protectorate, if that's what you mean."

It was a bold lie. I waited.

Rachel paused, and I could see her turning something over in her mind. She seemed to flicker in front of me like an image from a distant signal. She'd made some sort of decision. The enormity of her hand as she pushed back her hair!

"So you're here as a linguist."

"That's right."

"And what does that mean?"

I continued with the story about *Tomorrows* which, in its own way, was true. "I'm looking into its origins."

"Why?"

"To learn the identity of the author," I told her.

I don't remember it this way, but listening to it on the tape there's a long pause. There's also the sound of a distant siren or drone. Rachel didn't respond, so I continued.

"There's no such thing as anonymous. Who wrote it?"

"Why do you care?"

"It's an important book," I said, "too important to remain anonymous. The version I'm looking for also has something like a commentary, supposedly, a narrative or report about the editing process, about how the book came to be."

"I've never cared," Rachel said. "In fact, I think it'd be awful to know. Do you remember the picture-book version in hardcover, the one for kids?"

"I never saw that one."

There was a sudden, shocking vibration and the lights hissed and flickered. Both Rachel and Paul glanced at the ceiling, as if to see through it, and then Rachel shut her eyes.

In those few days with her she did this several times, closing her eyes for no apparent reason, sometimes for just a few seconds, sometimes for longer. I wondered about it then and I still wonder why. To rest them? To pause the world for a moment? Weirdly I didn't feel shut out when she did this. If anything, I felt closer to her, maybe because I was able to observe her in those moments without feeling self-conscious. Without any feeling at all except the ease and happiness of being there with her.

Suddenly a little orange fox or fox-like animal just like the one from earlier at the hotel windowsill appeared, crouching in the dusty doorway of Fletcher's. It observed me, flicking its yellow tail, the hair on its spindly back standing up. I felt a surge of feeling coming from the animal, a fuse-blowing surge (*manic affect* Charlotte would call this) but it wasn't supposed to come from animals, and it took me by surprise, momentarily making me vulnerable before Rachel, whose own affect I was finding so difficult to plumb.

*

Giant Paul, meanwhile, was wheeling in from a back room or a storeroom some enormous contraption which turned out to be a pinball machine. On a rusted dolly he slotted it into a space outlined by dust or sand against a wall and then proceeded to lie down on his back on the floor and shimmy his way beneath the machine, presumably to plug it into the wall. While he was beneath the machine the phone at the bar began to ring and with a kick of his large black-booted foot he signaled for someone to answer it, and so I did. *1638 McNichols* the voice said, and then silence.

"Well?" the barman asked from beneath the machine.

"Line went dead," I said, the sort of on-the-spot lie that will accumulate like sediment in your mind until there's no way to know why you said it except through the eyes of a stranger, like a priest at confession or a therapist, far into the future. "Tell me what you know about McNichols," I said to Rachel, retaking my seat at our table.

"McNichols!" she said, "that's the street *we're on!* McNichols and Livernois!" The phone rang again and no one answered it.

The gathering night collecting in the corners of Fletcher's made it seem, for a while, as if we were in some sort of extended cut of a documentary that suddenly reversed course and became a surrealist film. The single window was aglow with a projected orange fire that made it seem as if the sun had been instructed to direct its rays right towards this bar. The door of the bar opened of its own accord, it seemed, and a kid on a silver bike with Day-Glo spokes popped a wheelie on the sidewalk outside, then came back and did it again.

Charlotte had warned me about little events like this—kids on bikes, the power cutting out briefly, phones ringing in the night but not sounding exactly right. She'd told me I'd need to be alert for repetition, for patterns, for clues that hinted at a larger structure.

The door closed.

Paul was struggling to balance the pinball machine, and I offered to help hold it up slightly as he unscrewed one of the legs to lengthen it. *Indiana Jones and The Temple of Doom: The Pinball Adventure.*

"Of the 12 modes, the *Steal the Stones* one is the hardest," he said, using a level, and then further readjusting the leg, "and within that, *Survive the Rope Bridge* is the most difficult.

If you complete all 12 modes, which practically no one does," he said, wiping his brow, "you get six balls at once."

The phone behind the bar rang again and Paul asked Rachel to answer it. It was mounted on the wall, a red rotary phone although it had a modern, digital ringtone and by the time Rachel got there it had stopped ringing. But then it started again and she picked up, took off an earring and pressed the receiver to her ear, listened, and then held the handset tight to her body. But you could still hear the whine of the drone, high-pitched and terrifying, screaming into her chest.

June 30, 1999

Antony,

Is this going to be a long one? Maybe. Probably. Hopefully.
I can see the sun coming up across the tops of the hills in
the distance and I can feel the sun's rays on my face before
they arrive just shutting my eyes.

I have to sleep on my back now.

How many times did Paul practice that "Mitchum's a
bum" line, I wonder? Knowing Paul, he didn't think twice
about it which was, of course, the whole point. To sound as
natural as possible. But still, it was important, that first line.
He had to get it right, Antony! Little things like that mattered
so much at the time! They seemed to matter. How to engage
you without making it feel like we had been thinking about
how to engage you?

Paul told me later that you fell so easily right into the
conversation that he suspected something but he stuck to
the script. I guess his thespian training as Pauline from high
school paid off, unless he was just acting about that too.

Could you tell, Antony, that Fletcher's wasn't what it
seemed? It wasn't just paste and cardboard, if that's what
you're thinking. And it wasn't exactly built just for you,
either, since you weren't the first. The cult flag and all the
rest weren't the real props, of course, but the whole point was
to get you to think they were. The real prop was Fletcher's
itself and to a greater extent Detroit, or at least the Detroit
that you saw. I don't know how much of it you learned from
Charlotte but the first trials here in the early 1990s—the first
wave—were real disasters. How to make a *second* city, a city
overlaying the original, but without changing the original?

It seemed to all be going so well until it wasn't. The failure had to be blamed on somebody and who knows why it was Paul but, well, it was Paul. Which accounts for the scars, partly. I was part of the second wave that was tasked with, as I've come to understand, *lesser* goals. Lesser goals, Antony! Just listen to that! *Lesser goals* than, what? Than replicating a city, or *seconding* it as they used to say. No one knows for sure—at least not anybody *I* know—details of how the first wave was supposed to work or why it failed.

We didn't know anything about how it was supposed to work other than: it didn't work.

Paul, when he was drunk, would sometimes allude to it when he'd show and tell about his scars, how the doubling had gone so well at first, Detroit as a double helix doubled on itself. But when it collapsed it collapsed big time, he'd say.

Big time. Can't you just hear Paul saying that?

So when I say the real prop was Fletcher's I hope you can see how pathetic that's meant to be. I guess the second wave had gone from replicating Detroit to fashioning these second-rate, cardboard-and-paste places like Fletcher's with their phony cult flags and pinball machines. It's strange how when nothing's written down, nothing's recorded, it seems more real, more distinct, and so that's how it is with what happened during the first failed attempt to make a parallel Detroit to trap people like you, from the protectorate.

*

Well the sun's been up for a while now. I was out of bed and now I'm back in it. Same old sheets. Same old body. Would you love me if I was old? An old woman? If my face was the same but older? If my hands were the same but frailer?

Veinier, bonier? If my scalp was drier? If my, you know, was the same but older? If you had to brush my hair at night? If I farted when I sat? If when you came into the bathroom after me you noticed the little detritus of my grooming?

Did you know that Paul was into deep time? Deep, geologic, time, man. Universal time. You probably caught that "hip to time" reference, or didn't you? I never cared for Easy Rider but then Paul, obviously, did. There's a re-cut version made by the Fisher Radicals— have I mentioned them yet or did you already know about them?—that has an ending so happy it could be interpreted as ironic, if you were on the protectorate's side, one where the guy in the pick-up truck misses and the film ends with Dennis Hopper's middle finger. There was a whole thing back around ten years ago with re-cutting movies and even re- staging scenes to play out differently, sometimes only slightly differently, not with dramatically altered endings like in *Easy Rider* but more subtle alterations like a new breakfast scene in *E.T.*, things like that that were pretty easy to re-stage and film. *Chariots of Fire* was another one, I think it was a new cafeteria scene that shifted sympathy a little bit in favor of one of the less likeable characters.

It's strange really, looking back on it now, how I used to think things like that mattered. I was obsessed with the little details and intrigues of our resistance and I suppose it was because I met Paul during that time that I stayed close to him even after we drifted apart in so many other ways. He had this habit of taking off his shirt in the summer sun when we'd work in the garden out behind the bar and I remember the flat brown moles like warped quarters and the little black hairs way down on the lower part of his back.

I could see the surgical scars on his chest. So here was this fact: Paul took his shirt off. But what to make of it? I wasn't used to having people like that take their shirts off in front of me, Antony! What did it mean? Did it mean *any*thing, or was he just doing the most obvious thing that men had been doing for thousands of years when they worked hard outside? Or was he just playing the role of that sort of man? Then I remembered he was Greek and I thought well, it's in the genes or whatever from men and women working the fields in Greece. He wasn't really in the best shape but I found him attractive anyway, his little rolls of fat that bulged at the top of his pants, the moles, the hair. What did he think *I* thought about him being shirtless, or didn't he? Maybe I was the weird one for thinking about it too hard.

Paul said the garden was fast time: you planted in the spring and harvested in the fall.

The woods were medium time.

Rocks of course were slow, deep time. But people, what were people?

July 22, 1999

Dear Antony,

It's morning and I feel like hell. Impossible to sleep. It got so hot last night I thought about dragging some cushions out to the balcony and sleeping there like I used to as a kid on our back deck. I wish you could have seen me back then, I was so shy. My mother said I didn't talk until I was five and then I didn't stop.

I wish I had warned you about the more radical of us. The Fisher Radicals. Or did I? I mean you knew about Yama. But did you know they were part of a more organized sub- group, a group that took their cues from Marinetti and the rest of that Italian Futurist gang who saw beauty—real beauty—in violence? In the violence of war and torn apart bodies? The speed of violence. The spectacle. What a cliché but God knows I was tempted.

They'd come around Fletcher's trying to recruit us with their worn-down slogans as if we'd never heard them before. Do you remember the kid on the bike? They'd send ones like him around just to let us know they knew where we were. Who knows, maybe that's when they spotted you, maybe the kid told them.

It's late now.

My blue pen ran out so I've switched to this. I have to believe that you're receiving these letters, obviously, or else I couldn't write them. If you are really in the hands of the more radical of us then God help you. It's so dark. There's a scrawny, dirty kid who imitates owls in this neighborhood so I can't be sure if what I'm hearing now is a real owl or the kid. Either way, it's soothing. I've warmed up some coffee in a pan. There's light in the sky. It's so soft and beautiful tonight from out on my little balcony where I can also see the small black bats making their jagged little circuits back and forth. They seem to be mimicking my thoughts, going here then switching direction suddenly and then going there. There's a woman somewhere in the building who plays a song that we—those of us active in the insurgency—used to associate with the protectorate. I know who it is because she sometimes hums it when she's taking out the garbage.

I sometimes wonder if you knew about us, about me and you. Knew our history, what we shared. From what I understand, probably not. I mean, would you have kissed me like that if you did? And those other things? Knowing what I know about you now, I don't think so, Antony. But still, I can't be sure. If you did know, when did you know?

I think about us all the time.

I think about where you are now, as I'm writing these words, and I think about where you will be when you're reading this. Or if you will be. God, is that cruel to say?

The owl kid is out in the open now, in the street beneath my window. He's looking. I'm sending you this letter with no proper ending.

August 3, 1999

Dear Antony,

I can't remember if I told you in the last letter about the scruffy owl boy coming up to my apartment. These days it's kids, mostly, who send messages and run errands for whatever's left of the protectorate and whatever's left of the insurgency. I didn't let him in, of course. You never do that. They always come with some nugget of information—just the smallest of things— in hopes that you'll pay for more. The owl kid is persistent. It's always a variation on the same thing, a few phrases from *Beyond Blue Tomorrows* that I always pretend not to recognize.

The other thing I wanted to tell you about is the weather, the way it brings sand in every evening. At night the light of the sky is so beautiful, Antony, so sparkly golden and then in the morning the soft sand coats everything. We don't know where it comes from. In the morning I awaken to the sounds of people shaking out their sheets and tablecloths and towels and clothes from their balconies. The street sweepers below. And now the giant, makeshift exhaust fans that blow the sand who-knows-where.

Oh, and my armpit hair has quit growing!

Is that gross to tell you? I tossed it in to make sure you're paying attention and reading my words carefully. Ha ha.

There are so many theories and counter-theories about where the sand comes from and what it means and there are even some who don't think it's sand at all. But I don't care anymore, Antony. What does it matter? We're all breathing it, whatever it is.

The least persuasive part of your cover story (isn't that the sort of phony language people like Charlotte used?) was the bit about being chair of a linguistics department. Am I right in remembering it that way because I don't think there's any such thing as linguistics departments, are there? English departments where people study linguistics maybe, but not whole departments. It was almost embarrassing the way you talked about it sort of under your breath in passing like you were afraid I'd ask you more about it and I was tempted, just to watch you squirm but I don't know Antony, I didn't want to. You probably didn't know but Charlotte has a very limited imagination and she'd already used the linguistics backstory a few years before you arrived, with someone else who didn't last as long as you.

I wish you could answer me. I know now that my letters are being delivered to where you are, but are you able to respond? If you could, what would you say? Are you the same Antony you were before they captured you at the church? Paul used to brag about the sorts of "measures" (his word) he took against people like you when he was part of that group but I never thought too much about it until you came along. I don't even know if the things he described were true. Well, you remember. That's the worst part. Now that I know you're getting these, the worst part isn't wondering what you'll think or how they'll make you feel but picturing you not being able to respond and wanting to respond.

There is so much more Antony! So much more.

Rachel

Antony

I MET RACHEL OUTSIDE FLETCHER'S THE NEXT MORNING
and that's when she took me to the greenhouse. The parts
I don't want to think about are coming up fast but I know I
have to and the tapes help. They make it real and strangely,
that's comforting. It's better than relying just on my memories and my imagination, where everything is blacker and
more terrible than the tapes suggest. One of the things I
don't want to think about again is the Colonel's suicide note,
a filthy document I received in my filthy cell. *Fucking fathers*,
is what the Commander would have said. Even though parts
of Rachel's letters were censored, they didn't censor anything
in his. They wanted me to feel the pain. They wanted me
to suffer.

Maybe I wanted to suffer too, and that's why I read it.

The greenhouse revealed itself slowly, in patterns. I remember panels of broken glass, greened and blackened-over
by scum and mold, in the weedy backlots. Rusted, flesh-like
strips of metal nailed to leaning telephone poles whose wires
had been slashed. The greenhouse seemed to have settled
there on a vast, flat open area that could almost have been
mistaken for a plain, the tall grass swaying like a weird in-
vitation that masked the danger of the greenhouse itself.

As we approached: enormous blackened industrial fan blades in a crooked stack like some sort of half-finished monument. The thick, sweet smell of honeysuckle. Tangles of old water hoses like nests. The close-by hum of something like insects or electricity. And then the crumbling circular brick wall, surrounding the greenhouse, as if that could keep anyone out. It seemed medieval almost, that wall, like a child's version of a moat.

"It should have been our biggest prize," Rachel said, leading the way, shielding her eyes from the sun with what looked like a crooked salute, "but it was abandoned days before we got here." And then, out of nowhere: "I think there's someone following us. It's just that feeling, you know? Can you feel it? I sort of like it."

Her green army jacket, decorated with silver safety pins along the collar. Her black hiking shoes, laced in bright red.

The thickness of her calves.

I'd switched out the boots Charlotte had assigned me for a pair of black Pingree sneakers, made in Detroit, Rachel assured me, back when Detroit still made things.

At one point the wall was just a heap of bricks, and that's where we crossed. I remember thinking that the marks I was seeing on the patches of clay-like, bare ground were the imprints of a horse's hooves. And then I wondered if I'd actually heard a horse, during the night, of if it was just a dream I was remembering. The greenhouse itself was large and pyramid shaped, with most of its glass windows still intact. There was a slight hum, a droning noise that I would forget to ask Rachel about until much later, after it was too late. For a moment I doubted everything and the absurdity of joining this stranger in this abandoned place struck me. I'd only met Rachel and yet I trusted her, despite Charlotte's warnings. She was silent as we approached the greenhouse, pushing our way through the dry weeds, and then through an opening where a door should have been.

The greenhouse wasn't the only structure on the grounds. There was another building, newer-looking, smaller, the complete opposite of a greenhouse, its windowless black walls like painted-over brick. On its roof was one of those old metal TV antennas, crooked over in a way that suggested the letter X. I remember feeling somehow that this building—this *other* building—was more important than the greenhouse and that what Rachel was really bringing me to see was the *other* building under the guise of a visit to the greenhouse.

Inside the greenhouse there was less plant life than outside and what plants there were, were dead. Rusted ferns in pots sat atop something like a butcher's block. What looked like blackened tomato plants in loose metal plant cages brought to mind, for some reason, enormous dead insects. There was a faint bitter smell in the air, fuel-like and chemical. The wooden tables and watering hoses were all pretty much intact. But the light was different, reddish, filtered through the glass panels at the apex which also were discolored.

In the center was a long black metal pole extending impossibly straight upwards and through the crooked opening at the top of the pyramid-shaped greenhouse. It appeared to extend out and above the greenhouse, although I hadn't noticed this from the outside.

Just two or three inches in circumference like a weird geometry and at the time, standing there with Rachel, I remember thinking how I'd learned in geometry class that there are infinite points in a line segment and how unreasonable—even insane—that seemed to me. The thing I wanted to know and the thing I didn't ask Rachel was: how far down does the pole go? I didn't ask because I was afraid she'd know the answer and blurt it out, confirming my suspicion that it was the insurgents, or some sect of the insurgents, who'd built the greenhouse rather than the protectorate. I imagined the pole went down deep into underground chambers where there was no light, forgotten and erased from memory and history because the people who built the chambers around the pole had been dead for so long.

"Be careful," Rachel said, taking my arm before I stepped in a puddle of something that gave off a bright silvery reflection, like a pool of mercury. "These stations. This was the model. It seems so fragile, right? So transparent with all the glass and the natural light. The illusion of being outside. Is there any structure less threatening than a greenhouse?"

But then there's this. On the tape you can hear the wind and the strange calling of a bird I'd never heard before.

Rachel reached out to touch the metal pole, I remember, gently, with the tips of her fingers. "Have you ever felt anything like this?" she asked. I put out my hand.

"Wait. Don't," she said. "Maybe you shouldn't."

"I want to."

I can picture how she smiled then, such a familiar but unknowable smile. So I touched it too.

My feet ached.

It was soft.

It had thought. The pole had thought.

It couldn't, but it did. I could detect it, ever so slightly. The pole was thinking.

*

I remembered touching a dead blackbird as a child, and then holding it in my hands.

Its small chest felt like clay. The Colonel had killed it with my pellet gun, why, I've never been sure. Maybe just to witness my reaction. Could he actually *see* the sick feeling welling up inside me?

"Go on," Rachel said, "push harder." She was sweating. We both were.

Rather than resist, it gave way when I pushed my thumb in, like cold putty, and when I let go it resumed its shape.

"What is it?"

"Wait. Now just put your palm on it, firmly, like this."

I copied her, and this time, rather than let me penetrate, it resisted, it pushed back, and the more force I used, the further away from the pole my hand was pushed, like that feeling of trying to hold two opposing magnets together as a child. My impression was that whatever the pole was, it had been here long before the greenhouse, which had been built and shaped around it. I wanted to say something, but what was there to say? That I could detect the faintest of thoughts coming from the pole?

"It's strange isn't it," Rachel said, "that something like this would go unremarked. What it was and what it meant and what its purpose was only became important when it mattered, when it posed a danger. Once the protectorate collapsed and left all this behind it became just a curiosity, and the remarkable fact of its existence means nothing."

The sun shining through one of the red glass panels fell on her face and made it movie-like, I remember, like a frame from one of those golden paranoid *noirs* from the 1970s. Thinking back on it I picture Rachel somehow knowing this and standing there in the light, holding a pose, letting me take in the full beauty of her face and closing her eyes like she sometimes did.

"What kind of danger?" I asked her.

"The most dangerous kind, the kind that doesn't hide itself."

I didn't have to wonder about why Rachel had really brought me there, to the greenhouse, to the pole. I touched it, as she asked, and it made no sense, as I knew it wouldn't. Of course I'd heard about the greenhouse from Charlotte, who also warned me that someone like Rachel would offer to take me to see it. The pole or whatever it was called was unexpected but only in its detail and specifics, as Charlotte had told me that something like this existed, a sort of signal tower constructed from a type of rare, naturally occurring clay and unrefined ferromagnetic metal.

It's hard to say precisely why, but I remember a wave of deep sadness there with Rachel. I can feel that so strongly now—it's more real to me than the greenhouse itself. I think it had something to do with the deception I was practicing, acting as if the greenhouse was a surprise to me, acting as if Rachel was a surprise to me. Which she was. But again, in a specific sort of way. I knew there would be someone, but not *this* someone. Who did I imagine it would be? Probably a person like Paul, a hulking insurgent. Even though I knew in my head that the protectorate's depiction and portrayal of the insurgents as primitives was completely constructed and inaccurate, I still couldn't fully shake that idea from my mind. And so the subtlety and grace of Rachel surprised me, thrilled me, even.

We walked slowly back to Fletcher's by way of Grand River Avenue, which at one time, Rachel said, had been a congested highway but which was now empty, five lanes of cracked and pot-holed asphalt tagged with the fading sigils of this or that breakaway insurgent group. The part of Grand River we were on was a makeshift landing strip for the new silent-running drones Paul's group was testing. The sun glinted off her safety-pinned collar. We cut through crooked alleys the rest of the way, some of them bound by tall wooden, vine entangled fences with loose and fallen gates stripped of their metal hinges and latches. The sky was deep blue and you could see, faintly, the moon, like a thin wafer. Soon the alleys gave way to a vast open space which looked from the distance like a meadow, but turned out to be an enormous parking lot unattended for so long that grasses and saplings had reclaimed it from beneath. We pushed our way through the weeds and came across remnants of the crucified straw X bodies that I would encounter again later, these so deformed by the elements that their shape held no meaning for me at the time.

I loved the way the air felt in Detroit, so different from northern California and Crescent City, where I'd been trained. I'd imagined the air being polluted in Detroit and even dreamed of it being rusted, particles floating in the evening sky to filter everything in a dull orange bloom and for a moment as I followed Rachel through the overgrown lot, I imagined the black pole back at the greenhouse watching us, watching us through a glass lens lightly coated in rust so that we appeared discolored and that all the information ever collected by the protectorate had been discolored like that, with nothing appearing the way it really was. I wanted to look back over my shoulder at the pole towering up through the pyramidal greenhouse but feared something Lot's wife-like happening, and then just as the thought formed, Rachel stopped, locked eyes with me, glanced back at the pole, and then at me, as if transferring her gaze—what she had seen—into me. It's as if I *had* looked back at the pole without looking at it. And then I remembered what Rachel had said about being followed by someone. It made the feeling that we were in the middle of some mystery together even stronger.

The lot narrowed and gently sloped downwards to a ravine with piles of crumbling red bricks and then a slate-tiled path that widened and then narrowed again beneath the canopy of towering elms of the sort that grew everywhere in Detroit before the disease that decimated them struck, and then we were back on the street where Fletcher's was and I still felt watched and yet despite that, I felt safe with Rachel, or if not safe, protected, and wondered if our journey to the greenhouse had served as some sort of warning or, instead, a cry for help.

*

"Can you help me?" Paul asked, and at the time I thought maybe it was a plea for help, a real *plea* of the existential sort. I considered Paul there in his plain, awkward largeness like a person who never quite mastered the extra-ness of his body. He seemed dilapidated and harmless and terrifying at the same time.

This was after the greenhouse, I think.

"I need you to deliver something for me. A set of keys. To a place not far from here, and I'll keep the drinks coming all night when you return, on the house. I'd deliver them myself but I can't in case of *that*," he said, nodding to the phone, and we both knew what he meant. He was more relaxed now than at the beginning and I wondered how much of that was a deliberate or connived strategy to put us at ease and how much of it was a genuine feature of his personality. The Colonel told me once to try to imagine my enemies as little children, the little children they once were. I tried this with Paul but it didn't work and I remember thinking that Paul had never been born *at all* but had come into the world in his own way, fully formed. The sound of Paul's voice on the tapes only reinforces that: I don't believe he ever *had* a child's voice.

Later, Rachel would tell me that Paul had had an operation a few years back to remove a metal fragment from his back, a fragment from a roadside bomb that had gone off about three blocks from here during one of the protectorate's sweeps. They successfully removed the metal but accidentally left something inside him, a small suction cup or suction tube. When he went back in to have *that* removed they found *another* piece of metal—a larger one—that hadn't shown up on the X-rays. The surgeon was bedeviled by it. Rachel said that's the word Paul used: *bedeviled*. The doctor told him it should have shown up on the X-ray. Actually, before he removed it he had the nurses wheel in an X-ray machine—this was while Paul was still unconscious—and take three X-rays, and even then, that metal fragment didn't show up. The surgeon said he was going to keep the metal fragment and study it because there's *no way* it shouldn't have been detected. Ever since,

Paul's been convinced, Rachel told me, that there are more of those undetectable metal pieces in his body, just waiting there in his flesh to activate or something. She also said that Paul curses the hugeness of his body because that means there's more mass for the metal to hide in.

"Activate?" I said.

"His word, not mine."

Paul fished from his pocket a ring with two green keys on it, separated by a small silver skull, tossing them in the palm of his enormous hand a few times as if to measure and judge their weight in ounces. (Roughly the weight of a mouse, I figured.) By this time the sun had set and the lights scattered about the place seemed to come up on their own, softly, and the feeling of the bar had changed somehow, very gently, very softly. It was like being in one of those elaborate aquariums, the ones that surround you as you walk through enormous rooms and tunnel-like structures with the fish all around you, the weird half- light softly shifting between various hues of green where just the slightest shadings give a different feeling and different meaning to everything. An *extra* meaning, somehow.

"Keys for who? We gonna get killed for this?" Rachel said, with no hint of humor.

"Of course not."

"Maimed?"

She was speaking for both of us now, sternly but in a sort of ironic way that bonded us (or so I thought) against the force of this gargantuan Paul-person holding the keys.

"They unlock a warehouse at Puritan and Wyoming," he said. "You'll meet someone around back and give her the keys."

"What's in the warehouse?"

He paused. The light had shifted yet again. "Supplies."

"And?"

"A box. The keys are also for that. But you shouldn't need to use them."

A thin layer of sand or something like sand had accumulated on the surface of the bar. There was a distant burst of gunfire. Then silence. Then another burst, this time closer.

The sand on the bar counter jumped. Paul's eyes darted to the door and then back to me. It wasn't the first time that I felt a tingle that suggested Charlotte was either watching or listening and I wondered if Rachel and Paul sensed it too.

Paul dropped the keys into Rachel's hand.

"Why don't you come with us Paul?" Rachel said.

"Can't. Not my kind of thing. Plus, the phone."

Not his kind of thing, Rachel repeated to me, while looking at Paul. "Then we should just stand him up against the 8 Mile Wall with a blindfold and a last cigarette and be done with it," Paul said.

"Hasn't there been enough division in this city already, Paul? Do we really need to divide Antony's soul from his body?"

Another round of gunshots that sounded like they were coming from the roof.

Rachel seemed reluctant to pocket the keys, as if doing so would finalize whatever it was we were about to do. I studied her sharply cut bangs and noticed that one eyebrow was bushier than the other. There were footsteps on the roof, then another gunshot, and then it was quiet. Paul walked calmly over to the door and locked it.

Rachel handed me the keys and I handed them back.

"We're in it *together* now Antony," she said. I also play that part of the tape over and over. *Together*.

Paul stared at me with dead eyes.

By this time, I think Rachel sensed or knew my real reasons for being in Detroit. And yet I was naive to think it didn't seem to matter and I let myself believe that there was no danger in what I was doing and that maybe the conflict between the protectorate and the insurgents had been exaggerated. For there I was, in their midst, this intractable cell of plotters against the protectorate whose days—from the little I'd witnessed—seemed as banal and unremarkable as mine, on the other side. I'd been trained by Charlotte to guard against what she called *reverse-sympathetic-identification* but I convinced myself I hadn't been there long enough for that to happen. Falling in love with Rachel was one thing, I believed, but what had that to do with blinding me to the so-called terrorist mindset of the insurgency itself?

In any case, the idea hung like a dirty curtain in my mind and the only way to step through that curtain cleanly, I felt, was to go along with what was happening with Rachel and Paul and the escapade with the phone call and the keys. And although the political apparatus that had tortured so many, and was then replaced by democratic protectorate, and was then overthrown again by the protectorate, all of us who answered to Charlotte knew very well that fragments till remained of the dissidents or insurgents tentacled through a few key cities like Detroit, waiting for the moment to re-assert themselves. It was a game whose rules were always changing and that seemed to be perpetual, making "real life" something that was always haunted by the game itself.

*

It's just that I couldn't tell when the game was "on" and when it was "off," leading to a confusion about authenticity itself. Was the spark between Rachel and myself genuine or merely another facet of the game? If I felt something for Rachel, some deep and powerful desire, how could I separate that from the game, which she, also, was likely playing? More troubling was the feeling that the game was in fact *preferable* to so-called authenticity, and that it gradually supplanted everyday, natural thinking and feeling, so much so that this everyday, natural thinking and feeling began to seem false and forced, just as the game had in the beginning. The roles we were playing—or that I assumed we were playing—had grown to such outsized proportions in our souls that true feeling seemed foreign somehow. Seemed wrong. And on top of that: if Charlotte had instructed me to play this role with Rachel, who had instructed Rachel?

Rachel and I stepped out of Fletcher's and into the Detroit evening, heavy and wet and green from a shower that had moved through. Although we had been to the greenhouse earlier that day, it seemed long ago. The bus stop across the street was deserted and I could see the moon rising against the gray buildings in the distance. It's hard to say in retrospect how it came to be that we agreed to go along with the nonsense with the keys, but I think it had something to do with neither of us wanting the night to end, a sense that each of us was after something more than just flirtation, but what that *something more* might be wasn't clear yet and maybe our weird little night would somehow illuminate the future for us and show us which path to take.

The immediate path was south, continuing down Livernois, past the purple painted cinder block New Christ Church with the cross hand-spiked to the outside wall and the structure bounded or trapped, it seemed, on each side by empty, charred, weed-filled lots and then another lot recently converted into a vegetable garden gone to rot. Across the street there was an elaborate, pink psychedelic mural with the word C A R E stenciled in enormous red letters surrounded by lions whose muscles were depicted as gears and wires and machine parts.

I remember there was a heavy, musky smell coming from the storm drains. A light mist had gathered just above the asphalt from the recent rain.

Rachel's boot had become unlaced again but I didn't dare stop her this time.

As we walked she passed the keys to me and asked if they felt right. I didn't need to ask her what she meant because they were lighter than regular keys, as if made out of aluminum. When she gave them over her hand touched mine and for one flashing moment I thought of us in a dark warehouse together. On the tape there's a woman's voice hollering down at us from an open apartment window across the street, and I remember her head silhouetted in a yellow light and then more figures appearing in other windows and there is no denying it felt like we were being tracked, watched. I sometimes wondered what we'd all do if we didn't have this civil war to keep us occupied.

Did Rachel too—did the insurgents—have something like affect mining? Could she detect in me what I detected in her: duplicity? fear? desire?

Was she picking up and translating my signals as I was hers?

"Is it true that Ford's name is the only American name mentioned in *Mein Kampf*?" I asked her.

"How would I know?"

We finally seemed to be approaching the end of the block and the streets lights, or at least some of them, flickered awake a few times and then came on, casting everything in a dull, desaturated orange.

Three dogs approached us, trotting down the middle of the street. One of them had yellow eyes that seemed to waver in its head.

Like the pole at the greenhouse, I could hear the dog thinking, too.

*

In the distance I could hear the thudding of fireworks and the faint drone of a helicopter. At the intersection of Livernois and Puritan we turned left and kept walking, the moon directly above us in a once-again clear sky.

Across the street was a gas station with glowing red letters and behind it another simple church. The next intersection was Wyoming Street and before I knew it we were standing before an enormous brick wall, the front of the warehouse, as if it had materialized only when we approached. The building—built very close to the street like a fortress—seemed to extend the entire distance of the block. I followed Rachel as we traced the wall around the block and then around the block again until we were back at the front of the building, although as far as I could tell there was no difference between front and back, a Möbius strip of a building although of course it wasn't that at all.

"The witches," Rachel whispered.

Two women in the near distance. One was sitting on an overturned plastic milk carton and one was leaning against a tilted telephone pole, smoking. A pale, yellow light spilled from the narrow door of an old brick building. There were fireflies or something like fireflies floating in the doorway like some sort of natural curtain. Both women were wearing black, with long black hair, and as far as I could tell, black-painted fingernails. In that moment they looked posed, as if anticipating our arrival. In fact, they appeared more mannequin than human; still figures against the backdrop of a still night. Pitted there against the warehouse wall they stared at me and I had a sudden, sick feeling that it was not I who had come to Detroit, but rather it was Detroit that had come to me, reaching out and tentacling me in ways so gentle and natural and inevitable I couldn't help—for that brief moment—but see the tableau before me as some elaborately concocted and staged event.

"Hey Rachel," the one leaning against the pole said, flicking her cigarette into the blank, empty street and stepping towards us. The other stood up and walked away.

"Hey Julia," Rachel said, and as she did she gently nudged me with her elbow as if to say, *play it cool, Antony, play it cool.*

The one Rachel called Julia looked at me and then back at Rachel. Her long, foamy dreads against her skin. Their whip-like length. Julia smiled and extended her arms wide as if to take in the whole of the night.

"All this darkness . . ."

"And yet still it's too bright, sister," Rachel said, as if completing an agreed upon code. "Julia's uncle founded the Detroit branch of the Black Panthers so don't fuck with her. Isn't that right Jules?"

Although she looked much younger, she must have been in her sixties from the stories she told. She carried herself like a person who had suffered and who had learned to mask that suffering with a certain sort of swagger. The swagger of something deeper and older than mere confidence. There beneath the street lamp, you could see that.

"Name's Nefertiti but people call me Julia."

"Of course," I said.

Then she continued: "Paul and his paranoia," she said to Rachel.

"*So* fucking paranoid. But if anyone has reason to be it's him, right?" They were talking to each other as if I wasn't there, which I didn't mind.

"Does he ever really *tend* bar?" I asked.

They laughed, at the same time.

"Yes, Antony, Paul is the *bar*tender. He's always been the bartender," Rachel said. "Always and always, forever and ever. Amen," said Julia.

"Lead us not . . . Deliver us from . . ." said Rachel.

"He, Paul, serves the wine, and the bread," said Julia.

Rachel: "For it is written, he will destroy the wisdom of the wise."

Julia: "Paul the destroyer, the barroom employer."

Rachel: "Let no man therefore judge you in meat, or in drink."

Julia: "Paul closeth and openeth the bar, built above the pit of hell."

Rachel: "Paul cometh as Pauline and leaveth as Paul."

Julia: "He is all the Pauls. The Paul of all."

*

I don't remember how we got back to Fletcher's.

Every few minutes the Indiana Jones *Temple of Doom* pinball machine played a cracked, distorted snippet of the movie's score and a bit of dialogue in a pre-programmed attempt to get someone to come on over and drop in a quarter. The dialogue rotated through "Wear your jewelry to bed, princess?" and "I'm allowing you to tag along. So why don't you give your mouth a rest. Okay doll?" and "Anything can happen. It's a long way to Delhi."

"Everybody thinks they filmed the first *Robocop* in Detroit, but most of it was in Dallas. But they really did film *Action Jackson* here. And *8 Mile*," Rachel said, to no one in particular.

"Who the fuck cares about *Action Jackson*?" said Julia.

"I care about *Action Jackson*," said Rachel. "'It was a regular fuck-o-rama at my place last night.' How could you not care about that line?"

"They only say things like fuck-o-rama in movies."

Julia had come around to my side of the table and now I was sitting in between her and Rachel. "The way my women have been forced to obey, to perform, to play a part, centuries of acting piled up on top of each other. Until now," Julia said. "No offense to you, Antony, but really your gender has gotten off with one of the biggest heists in world history. Isn't that right, sister?"

She turned her attention to Rachel, who winked.

"That's right," Julia continued, "pussy heist! Those days are over, brother! A fantastical heist of epic proportions which allowed you to have your cake and eat it too. Not that I blame you—what a Goddamned pleasure to eat pussy and to be eaten, no matter whose mouth, whose tongue, and when each day brings more and more bloodshed and terror, what happiness it is to lay back at night beneath the soft lights and go at it. One thing that all the political theory in the world can't erase is the pleasure of a good orgasm."

"I never meant . . ." I tried to say.

"Put a sock in it, okay?" Julia said.

Paul was now wearing an expensive looking white shirt, sleeves rolled up. He was feather-dusting the vodka bottles on the shelves and spacing them apart exactly, actually using a wooden ruler. When he was done he stepped back, folded his arms, and surveyed the shelves in their symmetry and order.

He turned to us and smiled.

August 15, 1999

Antony,

It's strange, isn't it, to think that so much of our lives was spent (wasted?) thinking about politics and culture?

But now is the time for thinking about babies.

I don't know who's reading this and so you'll just have to see them for yourself someday. They. Are. Magnificent.

The entire arc of my life, basically, has been in the service of other people's ideas.

And yet, until recently, until I began changing, I'd never thought of it that way. Once I'd learned to see the world through an ideological lens there was no other way to imagine seeing it. What is that way for you, wonder? We didn't have enough time to talk about that. It's hard to disentangle how everything—how every way of seeing—got so wrapped up in politics. It all seemed so urgent, so real, at the time. I remember first meeting Paul and how the confidence of his ideas was so overwhelming and seductive and how I believed that he was merely expressing my own ideas, ideas I'd already been forming for a long time. I suppose that's why it never felt like I was following. I was leading. Paul—and—merely amplified what I already thought. They made it coherent. Gave it shape and purpose. Converted it into action,

Was it like that for you too, I wonder? Was coming to Detroit your own idea? Of course it wasn't. We knew that. But once it was proposed you felt like it might have been.

And then later you were sure it was. I know that feeling. I still have it and to this day can't untangle what were my own ideas and the ideas of Paul and the others.

(The owl kid came back last night, skinnier than ever. He has the face of a dog. He hooted at me as if he knew I called him the owl kid.)

It felt so good to despise you and lust for you at the same time, Antony! How can I say that. And yet there it is!

Even when we got to know you we never forgot why you had come and what you stood for.

The trick was that we had to believe—really believe—that we loved you and trusted you. You have no idea, Antony, how long it took us, the years of training, to make it so that we could slip into self-delusion so completely so that there was no way someone like you could detect it. If we were to trick you we had to trick ourselves. And so whenever you were in our presence we really loved you, all of us, even Paul. There was no way you could detect we were faking because we weren't, at least not in those moments.

Do you still feel the weight of the greenhouse I wonder? Do you still sense it watching you?

The panopticon. It turns out we all—your side and my side—read and studied the same theorists. Did you think you were the only ones who read Foucault's *Discipline and Punish*? We read him too, but for different reasons, not to exercise power, but to resist it. Your side read it as a blueprint for control, for getting others to internalize the very rules and codes of behavior used to subject them while our side read it as a critique of power. We didn't want your protection! As if we needed it—the protectorate. Who came up with that name anyway?

But none of that matters and that's not why I'm writing. There's something about the greenhouse I didn't tell you.

I couldn't tell you.

Not then and I shouldn't be telling you now but I have nothing left to betray except myself. The greenhouse was a ███████ system but not in the way you imagined. At the time I was worried it was all so obvious that you'd see right through it, like I'd suspected you'd seen through Paul and maybe even me and maybe even the whole system. I had to pretend to be as ignorant about the purpose of the pole as you and that meant trying to see it all through your eyes, and this transference—letting my senses go so I could experience the greenhouse through yours—was something I'd trained for years to do, just like loving you.

I had to love you for you to believe I loved you. It wasn't about touching the black pole.

There was no significance to that. It didn't mean anything. Antony! It was *getting* you to that spot.

To that exact spot. It wasn't the pole that threatened you but rather what came from beneath. To stand with your two feet at that exact spot, that was what I had to do. Because what happened to you when you touched the pole had nothing to do with the pole. The pole was nothing. What happened to you came from beneath your feet. Oh Antony can you forgive me?

You can't.

I won't let you forgive me. I won't let you.

It's no use explaining how it worked anyway—not in a letter. They'd never let you see it. I don't even know if you're seeing this.

All I can say is that's why you're there, in your little prison.

Because I lured you, you stood there long enough to touch that stupid fucking pole which was just long enough for them to take your ███████████████.

And now look where you are.

Antony

IT WAS STRANGE THE WAY THEY TALKED ABOUT THE
Fisher bombing, the event that had come to define the difference between our side and theirs. I'd avoided the pile
of rubble on Jefferson that had now become a memorial, a
scar that served as a reminder—for the insurgents—of the
protectorate's brutality. At least that's what I thought, what
Charlotte and the others had led me to believe. But here
on the ground among them I realized how poorly I understood it all, and that the collapse of Fisher Theater on that
day with all the elementary school children inside wasn't
viewed just as a singular atrocity, an act of mass murder,
but also as a sign of something bigger, bigger even than
the conflict itself. As part of our training, Charlotte had
showed us graphic pictures of the aftermath, the crushed
bodies and torn limbs of seven and eight year olds who'd
been at Fisher that day to see a play. I remember the girl
in the pink coat, her leg severed but the rest of her body
otherwise perfectly natural, as if she'd been taking a nap.
And I remember the grotesque image of one of the play's
performers still in her pirate costume looking bloody, her
face half-crushed, as if she'd been slain in an actual pirate
battle.

But it turns out that for Rachel, Julia, and the others, the significance of Fisher wasn't only the fact of the 43 crushed bodies or the bomb that brought the building down on them but that it represented a shift in the protectorate's thinking, a shift all the more alarming not because it happened, but because it had happened with the protectorate *first*. Why, they wondered, had the protectorate arrived at this point of inhumane thinking before the insurgents? If the conflict had always been evolving towards this type of murderous event, then what evolutionary leap (*epistemic leap*, Julia would call it) had happened on the other side? There was even a hint of jealousy when Fisher came up, as if the protectorate had pulled ahead not in the conflict itself, but in *thinking* about the conflict.

Flash. Julia was holding a small camera. Pre-digital. She thumbed the little plastic black dial to forward the film to the next frame until that satisfying *click*. *Again*, she said, as if we'd posed the first time. Rachel leaned in and before I could react there was another flash.

"Now you do me," Julia said, holding the camera out. "You take it Antony. Just press here."

She moved over and stood beside Julia.

In the flash I caught something at the back of the bar, some figure. A stain.

A shadow.

After the flash, it was gone. *Let's take another one*, I said, and this time I looked beyond them, to the back of the bar and there it was again, briefly illuminated, a shrouded figure melting into the far wall. I felt sick, I remember that, and went to the men's room, whose yellow tiled walls looked to have been recently scrubbed of graffiti.

Above the urinal, in sharp black marker, was the usual shark about to bite a penis doodle, except this shark had a thought bubble above its head that read, AM I ALREADY DEAD? It didn't really make sense and it wasn't funny or witty; if it was a joke or a play on words I didn't get it. As I was washing my hands there was a slight vibration, like a nearby door had shut, and I heard the low, whispered voices of who I assumed to be Rachel and Julia in the women's restroom filtering through the thin wall and a shared vent.

I watched my face in the mirror as they talked, unshaven, dark circles, my skin chalky under the fluorescent light, and I only caught snippets and phrases from next door: *supplies... tomorrow night at the latest... the field behind warehouse six... should we...* and then the talking stopped and a soft metallic, clinking sound rattled around from the air vent above my head like something had rolled from the women's side of the vent to the men's. I stood up on the toilet bowl—each foot carefully on the outer porcelain rim—and reached my fingers up to the vent and worked them through a gap and sure enough there was a small object. I took it out, rinsed it off in the sink.

A red marble.

Such a simple, common thing, and yet I had not seen one for a long time, probably going back to when I was a small boy at my cousin's in Kentucky, playing marbles on the wide-planked kitchen floor as the goats brayed out back. I dropped it in my pocket.

There was a gentle rap at the restroom door, followed by the barman's voice. "You alright in there, hombre?"

I opened the door and there he was, healthy looking again, recovered, as if whatever dark cloud had passed over him was long gone.

"The sisters think it's time I fed you."

It was the first time Paul had called them sisters, and the

first time he'd spoken to me so informally.

"We were worried that something ate you in there," said Julia, from back over at our table. Rachel was sitting next to her, her legs crossed, twirling a sliver ring on her pinky, and between them was a paper menu. "We're thinking of ordering a pizza. There's only one place that delivers this early and luckily that's the best place around."

The marble was in my pocket where I imagined it glowing like a warm ember, a sort of secret, dangerous connection between me and something else, something vaster, something unknown but wanting to be known and I had to make a concentrated effort to keep in mind why I had come to Detroit in the first place: not to loiter at a bar running nonsensical errands with strangers to abandoned warehouses to deliver messages but rather I'd come here to annotate an important document from the iron-grip era of the protectorate back when its will seemed inviolable.

The supplies, as it turned out, were crates of drones, small drones that needed to have their propellers attached. Like the Indiana Jones pinball game, the drones were about one thing and one thing only: knowledge. Rachel and Julia and Paul knew this, and *I* knew this, and the *Commander* who had sent me, *she* knew this, but did any of us know that the others knew? The drones had been a common weapon deployed exclusively by the protectorate during its first era, and then quickly adapted by the insurgents, so it was no great surprise that that's what was happening here in Detroit—this drone activity—which is what snagged my thoughts: why send me here to discover something as obvious as this?

While we waited for the pizza Paul razorblade-opened one of the cardboard boxes that had been delivered from the warehouse. He wriggled on a pair of thin latex gloves and gently lifted one of the drones out of the Styrofoam popcorn. It was a small contraption, about the size of a hand, with a clear, small dome on its belly side that I assumed held a camera. From another package he spilled out about a dozen or so small, colorless, plastic propellers. He snapped four onto spindles that shot up vertically from the drone, and then held it up in the air like a kid with a toy plane.

The marble felt warm in my pocket. The wind picked up. My feet were burning up. My legs felt weak. I could hear what sounded like dry leaves or sand blowing against the outside window.

I wanted to ask who the propellers were for but my mind was already swimming with too many variables and I felt lightheaded suddenly, and in the end it seemed easier just to wait for them to tell me. As Paul continued to attach small propellers to the drones, Julia stood over at the *Temple of Doom* pinball machine, while Rachel re-straightened bourbon and whiskey bottles on the glass shelves behind the bar.

*

"I think it's time," Julia said and disappeared into the restroom and came out with a small leather backpack and tossed it over to the bar, where Paul pulled it across to himself right away and unzipped it. With a resigned look on his face Paul surveyed the drones with the new red propellers.

"The drones," he said, without even looking at me, "are here only for two, two-day periods, twice a year. You happened to walk in here yesterday, during one of those periods. We're just one stopping point for them during their long journey. At each place, they're modified. Certain parts changed out for others. We're the propeller station."

I expected him to continue but he stopped.

"Who are they for? Why the red propellers on only some?"

"How could we possibly know where they're headed? We can't know, of course. Don't want to know. Just that they're going to our side. The red propellers are on the ones that have to make it through to the end, no matter what."

"Make it through?"

"Relax, Antony," Julia said.

She handed me one of the small plastic drones.

It felt like nothing in my hand, as light as a thought.

*

"There are people," Paul said, having attached the red propellers, "people working at this very moment—to restore the protectorate, and if you don't think it's true you should take off those blinders and have a good look around."

He said this with the kind of disdain I remembered from the Colonel's voice. With an uncharacteristic flourish, Paul placed shot glasses on the bar, filled them with a clear liquid from an unlabelled bottle and said he wanted to make a toast. Behind his eyes there was what I can only describe as a blankness. We raised our glasses. "To the unwritten future," he said. And then, "let's hope it's worthy of our plans." As I drank to whatever it was he meant, I got the feeling even he didn't know. It felt like some misplaced line from a play nobody could remember the name of.

This also reminded me of the Colonel, who often talked in code like that, or at least to what a child's ear sounds like secret code, one that only gradually translates into meaning as we get older. In terms of the Colonel, what I came to understand as disdain first presented itself to me as the language of camaraderie, a sort of secret shared humor between us. It wasn't until I was 12 or 13 that it took on a darker shade, something tinged with sarcasm, as in *As smart as you are you can figure it out*, and then, later, as disdain.

Either the Colonel had lost the ability to be subtle or I was hearing the code differently, but by the time I was in my late teens he'd stopped engaging me altogether, dismissing me with pronouncements like *You can't see because you don't want to see*, or *Your generation is too shallow to care*.

The funny thing is I believed he was right and thought he was trying to engage me. I *didn't* want to see.

My generation *was* shallow.

Who but the Colonel was brave enough to tell me? But why wouldn't he give me a chance to respond, to engage him, for in truth I took what he said not so much as an insult but rather as a sociological generalization. It was true that my generation avoided, it seemed to me, deep and potentially confrontational conversations about religion or politics or art, perhaps out of a feeling of futility. And was this shallowness also responsible for my jagged, painful relationship with the Colonel, whom I wanted to love?

I knew of course that Paul was right. I was one of the people working to "restore the protectorate," wasn't I? There was something paranoid and thrilling about the Albanian story Julia told me, and the drones, and the grotesquely oversized Paul, and the cryptic toast nonsense and the nonsense about going to fetch the "supplies" and all the rest of the crazy nights and days with the three of them, and yet at least they seemed the right sort of people, I thought at the time, people on the right side of history, or at least with a sense of history, and perhaps even they could be useful to me in my *Tomorrows* investigation somehow, providing some kind of counterbalance to my own obsessions, my own guilt.

Was I afraid that I would find myself there, in those pages? The words of the Colonel, the protectorate's theorist of repression and torture. Is that why I was putting off anything to do with *Creatures*, spinning my wheels at Fletcher's, a place that seemed to straddle some threshold between *being and becoming.*

We spent the rest of the night at Fletcher's, talking. I slept a little bit. Paul offered me use of his "craftsman shower"—that's what he called it—in the way-back part of Fletcher's. It was nothing more than a sturdy garden hose with a sprinkler nozzle attached dangling from a ceiling beam. The water was warm, though, and I imagined the hose snaking down to a pitch-black sub-basement where, lying coiled next to an old boiler, the hose had a ready supply of warmed-by-hell water. I scrubbed my face and dried my hair in the whoosh of an old porcelain hand dryer. I must have slept after that because the next thing I remember it was morning and I said, with no idea or plan in mind, "I'm going for a walk."

"A walk?" Julia said. "What time is it?"

"Does it matter?"

Rachel and Julia shot each other a look, and then together looked at Paul.

My ankles and were burning up again and then it dawned on me: the boots Charlotte had instructed me to wear were meant to serve a purpose. To protect me. At the time I had no idea that the greenhouse had been contaminated and that I'd been standing on tainted ground. It was only later, after my ordeal, that I learned that's how they'd tracked me to the church: the soil on my shoes. Charlotte's boots had been meant to inoculate me from that, although who knows if they would have worked.

"What do you think Paul?" Rachel asked. "Do I need his permission?" I said.

"Not permission, counsel. Guidance."

"Rachel's right," said the Paul-person, "I can tell you the best route to take."

He pulled out a wrinkled paper placemat from behind the bar and began to draw a map with a blue ink pen. After a minute or so he flipped it around and said, *you are here*, which he marked with a star, and then talked me through the dotted line he had drawn that was a rough, zig-zagging square stretching several blocks and ending up back at the bar.

Then he took it back, made a few more markings, and slid it back across to me.

"Avoid these places," he said, pointing his enormous hotdog finger to one of the three places marked with a filled in blue circle.

"Even in the daylight?" I asked.

"Especially in the daylight," he said.

I considered the warning areas, but they weren't that well marked.

"Nothing around here opens 'til noon," Julia said, looking at her nails.

"If you see dogs, or packs of dogs, don't stare at them in the eyes. They won't hurt you but don't stare at them," said Rachel. "Everybody learns that as a kid but then forgets."

"Thanks," I said, "I won't be long. Will you be here when I get back?"

"Of course," Rachel and Julia said at the same time.

The noisy pinball machine kicked to life suddenly and then died just as quickly.

The marble in my pocket vibrated, as if trying to express itself somehow. I could feel its color somehow, blood clot red.

I thought of Charlotte and her pale skin. The One Who Comes In the Night.

The shrouded figure illuminated by the flashes.

And with that I folded the map, put it in my pocket, and walked out.

September 10, 1999

Antony,

I got to thinking about what I wrote earlier: how much did you know about the Fisher bombing? I don't mean to accuse you Antony—I'm not saying you knew more than you let on—but now that I have time I wonder. In the wake of the bombing all our darkest, most paranoid assumptions about our foes hardened into facts, facts written in shattered children's bones.

Protecting us was the last thing the protectorate was doing. But until Fisher the prospects of what were at stake had never been so clear. What I mean to say Antony is that Fisher gave clarity to the shape of the protectorate, real vicious shape.

Antony, when this is over and you are free (you will be free) I want you to come back to me whole enough to understand these things, whole enough to love me still despite . . . us. It's not our fault who we really are to each other. It's not our fault we fell in love.

Rachel

Antony

I HEADED NORTH ON LIVERNOIS, IN THE OPPOSITE
direction Rachel and I had walked on our way to the warehouse.
The sun was up, and the street was quiet.

I passed a closed bicycle shop whose sign said it had been
established in 1938.

I tried to imagine what this street would have looked like
then and with a little imagination you could see the old elegance in the architecture of some of the buildings and in the
wide, boulevard feel of the street. Outside Simply Casual, a
clothing store, an elderly woman in an old house dress was
sweeping the sidewalk.

There was a grey squirrel in the tree above her making
its guttural rattle noises and flicking its tail.

It's gone dark.

One note, forever.

A defaced police car with a smashed fender sped by with
its lights flashing but no siren. A neighborhood—Sherwood
Forest—of slim, elegant red-brick houses with leaded windows and turrets, as if.

As-if turrets, I thought. As-if what: some medieval horde
attack? Turrets! A Citgo station, I remember that, its faded
red sign covered in bird shit.

A derelict bar called The Reason Why, its sagging over-hang propped up by a couple of warped two-by-fours.

At the corner of Livernois and 7 Mile I turned right and out from an empty lot came three brown, collarless dogs, tails wagging. They seemed harmless enough, but then I noticed that one of them, the smallest one, had some-thing attached to its tail with a wooden clothesline clip, a red fragment of folded paper, like construction paper, and while I was tempted to reach down and relieve the dog of the clip its eyes caught mine and I remembered what Rachel had said. In any case the dogs trotted off across the deserted street and that's when I noticed the church with the fallen over steeple.

I checked the placemat map and sure enough there was a blue ink dot at a crudely sketched church at just this loca-tion. The church was brick, and everything *except* what was brick about it was rotten or crumbled: the windowsills, the makeshift handicapped ramp, and apparently the steeple, which had fallen directly toward the street, not completely detached from the main structure, its cross-less tip pointing like a tank turret. *Avoid these places*, Paul had said and yet wasn't that precisely why I was here, to dive into the dark, into the unknown, into danger?

It wasn't lost on me—in fact I had anticipated it—that a dilapidated church figured prominently in *Beyond Blue Tomorrows* as the place where the insurgents met, and were ultimately betrayed, and, as rumor had it, portions of the story itself were written here sometime before the insur-rection. I remember how when I was a boy the Colonel had threatened me with Detroit, as in *with one call I can have you sent to Detroit you know*. Back then, at least as I remember it, Detroit was known for many terrible things but especially the serial killers of children. I kept a morbid tally of them in my diary—11, 12, 13—out of fear and adolescent fascination. I don't know if the Colonel's threat—delivered casually over breakfast and out of the blue after several days of behaving, I thought, like an incredibly obedient son—had anything to do with the string of killings. Strangulations, as I recall. Was the Colonel aware that I associated Detroit with the murder of children like me?

A beat-up, white, vinyl-topped Lincoln Town car went by slowly, its windows rolled up. It slowed to a stop in the middle of the street about 100 yards in front of me, and then its reverse lights came on and it began inching backwards. I walked straight ahead, towards the car and as we approached each other the rear right passenger door window was rolled down and from the shadows of the car's interior an arm extended holding a flyer which I stepped over and took. It was a crude, mimeographed flyer in black and white for a band called Yama for one of their shows at The Old Miami on Cass Avenue.

"We're into deep history," the voice from the car said. "The show's tonight, you got anyone else you can give these to? A dangerous band for dangerous times."

"Give me a few more and I can put them up at Fletcher's." The hand came back with a few more flyers.

"Fletcher's?" the voice said. "The place at Six Mile and Livernois, used to be called Grandy's? Triple o from way back."

He said this as a statement more than a question. The sun was now up now high enough to light the street and glint off the motel windows further down, and the windows of the few cars driving by. The Riviera was missing its second 'i.'

"Was called Grandy's until Grandy died. Deofol took over and then it was Deofol's until Deofol died. Then it was Pruitt's until Pruitt died. Then, let's see, Dixon's until Dixon died. Hmm. Then Greene's until Greene died. Then, if I'm remembering right, Spike's until Spike died, then Spike's again—a different Spike—until *that* Spike died. Fletcher took over and now it's Fletcher's. Someday it'll be something else and then it'll be Something Else's."

There was low laughter from the car.

In the distance a dog barked.

"*Paul* Fletcher?" I asked

"The one and only," the voice responded, "the big man. Former top dog. Did a lot of damage in his day, isn't that right?" the voice said to someone else in the car. The front window rolled down and another arm came out and gave a thumbs up, as if in response to the voice from the back.

"Damage how?" I asked.

"You know Paul Fletcher? If you knew Fletcher you'd know about the damage. And if you knew the damage you'd know Detroit. See? Fuck, man. No one told you about that address? 000 Livernois? The address of a Goddamned tomb."

The dogs came back trotting down the middle of the street toward the car, the one with the clothesline-clipped tail leading the way. Then another, larger pack came out from an alley behind them and the smaller pack turned, in unison, and their tales stopped wagging.

"Them dogs," the voice from the back seat said, "they act like they own this place."

The larger pack fanned out across the entire street and began moving forward, as if some sort of strategic canine offensive was underway and it was absurd to behold there on the sunny morning street. But before anything dramatic happened the smaller group bolted like flushed birds and scattered into the alleys and rather than give chase. The larger pack just re-gathered itself, tails wagging, and turned and headed, loping casually, back from where they had come.

"Anyway, see you at the Old Miami," the voice from the car said, hand extended. We shook hands.

"If you come just tell the guy at the door 'Pelham one two three' and he'll let you in, no cover. Oh, and if you see Fletcher, tell him 'Chu Chu remembers.'"

The voice from the front laughed, and then his hand shot out as a clenched fist that turned into a wave and the car slowly pulled away, its windows rolling up and the sun now warming the pavement, the street once again empty, and the distant, unmistakable whine of a drone, moving across the sky, watching or pretending to watch.

What difference did it make?

Back at Fletcher's I showed Rachel the flyers, but didn't tell her, at least not yet, what the guys had said about Paul Fletcher. *They don't want to talk to me*, I thought, for some reason that I can't remember, but I was wrong and it was Julia—who was now wearing a pretty short jean skirt—who was most interested in the men who gave me the flyers and who asked me if I'd gotten a look at their faces. *Were they brothers? Were they soul brothers?* she asked. I told her that, in fact, one of them was but that I hadn't really seen their faces, and she laughed and said, *That's because they don't have faces.* I know how silly it sounds, but she was so beautiful when she said that, so beautiful that it negated the real faceless woman I'd just seen.

Paul loped in from one of the back rooms and carrying a small, dark green burlap duffel bag that he set on the bar, unzipped, and proceeded to turn inside out. He began to sew—with a needle and red thread—something into the duffel bag, something which turned out to be a small piece of fabric of the same color as the duffel bag, a pocket into which he placed one of the red propeller drone blades. He sewed the pocket shut with the same red thread and turned the duffel bag right-side-out. He came out from around the bar with the bag and set it down at our table and I wanted to ask, *don't any customers ever come in here? don't you have a business to run?* But instead it was he who spoke first, saying something like *if one of you doesn't deliver this back to the warehouse there will be shit to pay* and it startled me because there was a threatening tone beneath his voice, his impossibly large, grapefruit sized fist there in front of our faces holding the bag like he was holding a slaughtered bobcat by its neck.

I was going to bring up Chu Chu but thought better of it, having no idea who or what Chu Chu was or what it might mean to him or how he might react. *We'll do it Paul but it's the last favor for a while,* Rachel said, implicating us all I felt, and although I certainly hadn't planned on agreeing to go on another nonsensical errand for Paul, I was also secretly thrilled to have an excuse to spend more time with Rachel and Julia. I'm not sure if it was because Rachel had detected that I had momentarily been stricken with Julia's aged beauty—which really had ambushed me—but beneath the table she began playing that old game of foot touching with me, tapping my ankle and then my shin with what felt like her bare foot. I pushed back playfully and waited and then started again, as Paul went over to check on the *Temple of Doom* machine and said, to no one in particular but loud enough so that we could hear, *I really do wish they could make a real temple of doom.* I had seen the movie but couldn't remember exactly what the temple of doom was, although I do remember the mine chase.

A real temple of doom.

Rachel's bare foot had moved up to my knee and I gently shifted my leg to push it away. In truth I wanted to hold her foot, which I imagined was cool and dirty, and have it in my hand beneath the table. In through the front door came a ragged customer in a baggy yellow sweat suit but no sooner had he crossed the threshold than Paul barked *not open yet.* It must have been early afternoon, maybe one or two, and there was a thunderclap and I thought of that line in *Taxi Driver*—Travis Bickle's weirdly flat, cold, menacing voice-over—where he says something about how *someday a real rain would come to wash all the scum away.*

The phone behind the bar rang a dull, underpowered ring and Paul just stood there, enormous hands to his side, staring at it as if willing it into silence or extinction, which didn't happen of course. Instead, the phone kept ringing and the Paul-thing kept staring at it, like someone staring into the eyes of those dogs they had warned me about and when it finally did stop ringing there was a palpable sense of relief, as if a spell had been broken or a curse had been lifted.

"Did you make it as far as the church?" Rachel asked.

"That's where I got the flyers for that band playing at the Miami."

"You mean Yama at The Old Miami."

"Right."

"Didn't Paul warn you about that church?"

"He put a blue dot there if that's what you mean," I said.

"Warning you," said Rachel. "I'm so sorry to say this but no matter how many times it's scrubbed or painted over or whatever, the 000 is . . . it's the end of, you know, the one who sees it. Those who see it are infected and end up on a dead man's list, you know. The triple zero is a grave whose parameters fit only between those three digits."

"I didn't go inside."

"But you stopped in front. And then the car pulled up. And then you were handed the flyers. My God. Were you...? Did you...?"

"And?"

"Doesn't that seem strange to you?"

I considered this before I answered. Paul was wiping down the bar, once again, as if anyone had used it, and I sensed he was listening to us, the man who, according to the guys in the car, had caused *a lot of damage in his day*. The man who, according to Rachel, believed he had *undetectable metal fragments* buried in his flesh.

"So what did they say when they handed you the flyers?"

The bar had gradually taken on a soft green glow as the morning crept by, and it seemed, or maybe it had always been this way, and this was the first time I felt I was on dangerous ground. I didn't really care to share what those in the car had said—what business was it of Rachel's?—but at the same time I was curious as to why *she* was curious.

"The guys in the car told me the church was full of devils and if I lingered too long there they'd possess me," I said.

The Paul-person slapped his wet towel across the bar, as if to kill a fly, and the *Temple of Doom* teaser dialogue popped on: *Anything can happen. It's a long way to Delhi.* Paul slapped his hand on the bar and, holding up the duffel bag with his other hand said, "The warehouse."

Putting it like this it makes it sound as if he was ordering us around, but that's not how it happened, not at all. Instead, I think we felt—at least I did—as if somehow he was showing us respect and paying us an honor by involving us in his deliveries, or whatever they were. Although I turned out to be wrong, I suspected at the time that there were no deliveries of drones or drone propellers or anything else but rather that we were sending messages, physical messages that couldn't be traced through telephone calls or e-mails or letters. The red propeller sewn into the duffel bag was indeed a message, but not of the sort I imagined at the time.

This was to be my third excursion from the bar into the city and yet it seemed as if I had been doing this for hundreds, thousands of years, as if these journeys to the warehouse and the terrible church had awakened some ancient genetic memory in me, in the part of me that was just stem cells and short tandem repeat duplications going back to something primordial, as if my entire existence had funneled me toward these past few days and the simple yet cryptic actions I was performing. Red propeller indeed!

I took the empty duffel bag from the bar while Julia and Rachel gathered their things.

"The same warehouse?" I asked Paul.

"The same one."

"And who should we hand it over to?"

"You'll see when you get there. There won't be any doubt about who it is."

The question ringing in my head, so loud that I feared Paul himself might hear it, was: *who was Chu Chu, and what did he remember?*

September 29, 1999

Antony,

So, I've been told that you're receiving these letters because of a change that occurred where you are and I've got to believe that you're reading them too, that you're able to read them. The change may be temporary so I have to write some things now because it may be our only chance. I've also been told that it's dangerous to keep writing to you like this, not for you, but for me. It would be too easy to say that I'm continuing to write out of guilt or even more, out of a sense that I deserve to be punished, too, in the way that you are being punished. I don't think you even know the half of it.

I wonder if you know, somehow, what we made together. See how it's not just us anymore? It's funny how intimacy changes history. No one writes about that, how two people coming together can create something so profound and yet so common at the same time. History is about war and death and heroism and yes, sometimes love, but it's silent about the small sweet steps leading to seduction and the fate of women like me who then carry inside them the tangible effect (or is aftermath a better word?) of that intimacy.

God I don't want to get too heavy on you Antony but now that I know these letters are coming through I want you to know what we made together, the little things (I can't tell you their names), the little creatures.

In retrospect it all sounds so neat and cruel and clinical, the way we pretended with you. But it was you, Antony, who came to us and that's the thing I keep telling myself. I want to scratch out every line I write and write it again so that it captures things the waythey really were, but that's impossible, isn't it?

I'm remembering not the events themselves but my memories of the events.

The whole propellers ruse for instance. We knew we needed some reason to keep you around and it was ███ idea to use the drone parts. But see even that's not really right. It wasn't so cynical as that. You wanted to be involved in a mystery and we all sensed that because we did too. It's not our fault, that feeling that history ran out on us and that our generation is stuck with making minor moves. All the real battles were fought a generation ago. All the ideas that matter have worn out and become over-used. Or is that just nostalgia?

Did anyone ever really believe in the protectorate? The insurgency?

Fighting over hand-me-down ideologies, is that all we have?

But I suppose none of that matters when you're chained to a bed in a black cement room. Is that what they've done to you Antony? Is that where you are? I don't want to believe—I won't believe—that my actions alone are responsible for whatever's happening to you right now. I can tell you that the way it was.

I took you to the greenhouse, it's true. And got you to stand there on that spot. But I knew something that the others didn't know: that the shoes you'd been assigned to wear would protect you from what was underground. The signals.

Oh Antony how was I to know? That you'd switched out your shoes (boots, I later learned) and were unprotected? I wanted to save you from the beginning, I did! I can say that now that it doesn't matter.

How could we have known that it wouldn't stop at kissing? Or maybe we did and that was the whole point? Thinking back, you can find inevitability in anything. Wasn't that one of the mantras those who sent you taught you—that it's the way you remember things that counts? That in order to be free of the past you have to remember it in the proper way, the way that aligns with the way you want the future to be? Paul got hold of some of those corny, over-zealous protectorate pamphlets with titles like *Memory as Antidote to the Future* and *Future Perfect Tense = Perfect Future* and *Square Waves Unrealizable in Box Formats*. Who wrote those?!? What morons! The idiocy! Or were they just bogus decoys to trick us into thinking your side was dumber than it was?

Remember Julia's scars? They were real but what she said about them wasn't. It's what the protectorate did to women like her when they were girls and it was dangerous of her to even show them to you but we needed to see your reaction. Did you believe her story, Antony, about how she got them? From "growing!" You showed no reaction which meant you weren't as complicit as we thought or else you'd been trained very well. It was, after all, the One Who Comes in the Night who'd sent you. Julia's scarring was from acid, Antony, and of course she didn't show you the ones between her legs, the ones that never have healed. How could you know, or did you? That's what we weren't sure about and it was her idea to show them to you like that, out of the blue, to see what thoughts drifted across your face.

Oh, Antony, your face. Love, Rachel

October 1, 1999

Antony,

I still wonder why you came, why you really came, to Detroit. We all did, at the time.

Sometimes when I'm alone here in the bed, lying on my back in the sun, my hands on my enormous belly, feeling them alive there just centimeters away, waiting for them to come, I shut my eyes and think back and wonder: what if the paths that led us both eventually to Detroit had been cleared for us a long time ago? No one wants to think they've just fallen into history, do they? I don't know about you Antony but it was unspoken in my family, when I was a girl, that underdogs were always right. In movies, books, palm games and whatever: the underdog. Truth to power. But what if that was wrong? What if the underdogs could, sometimes, be the bad ones?

Love, Rachel

October 9, 1999

Dear Antony,

They are here.

They are beautiful.

I haven't named them yet, is that strange?

I don't want to jinx them with permanence just yet. It's too early. They curl and uncurl at the same time and I feel like they already know they have each other but that's impossible, right? Do they even know they exist? They must. And they are so hungry. Julia is helping me with them, but she is so different now. Not the Julia you knew.

How can fingers be so small?

I wanted to tell you something else about Paul's sister Zoe, how after Paul told me that story about her scar he also told me something else, that she feared the cult had followed her out to Michigan, tracking her. Whether Zoe meant actual cult-people following her or that she was being monitored, he didn't know, but that's when he realized, he said, how similar he was to his sister, whom he'd never really known. I asked him similar in what ways and he said that both of them were attracted to power. For Zoe it was more intimate and personal in the form of the cult, a small circle bound by one charismatic leader and having access to that power, even just by association, gave her a feeling of power, Paul said, while for him, he said he realized he was attracted to larger systems of power, a sort of impersonal power. He told me all this after we got back from the Michigan dunes.

He also said that Zoe had, as part of the cult initiation, been witness to a drowning.

They'd taken a woman to a farmer's field and drowned her in the shallow water that had gathered there after a storm. It was only a few inches deep, Zoe said, and afterwards everyone had to kneel and touch the back of the drowned woman's head, putting their palms on it one-by-one. Zoe told him that her head was still warm and that one of the reasons she couldn't concentrate anymore was because she could still feel that warmth in her hand. I'm telling you this because I know how curious you were about Paul. I don't know if this helps you understand anything or not or whether or not it explains that sadness he carried around with him but I wanted to tell you because it's one of the things that attracted me to him and why I agreed to the whole Fletcher's scenario.

While you were here you saw the whole operation, pretty much. The way Paul runs it, at least. He's hardly the only one. You saw the exchanges, the elaborate nonsense set up to disguise some very simple but vital ███ . You can pretend you don't know what I'm talking about, that's okay. You thought that Julia and me and maybe Patti were witches; pretty funny.

Or that we were pro-pussy and anti-cock.

Maybe you thought we were revolutionary or insurgent witches and that we've got this weird thing going to cast a spell on people like you, people who still support the protectorate. God!

Did you ever hear or did I ever tell you the full story about Patti and Psycho Femmes? Patti dyed her hair red, just for you. Her background's in psychology and what she learned from your initial reaction to seeing her in the wheelchair is beyond me but she said it confirmed what we thought about you based on your profile. Patti's parents worked for the protectorate. Her dad was just a clerk but her mom was an informer—how exotic that sounds—who wormed her way into some of the book clubs here in Detroit. But the punk thing is real. Patti was in a band called Psycho Femmes and they even played with Iggy Pop a few times down at the Blind Pig in Ann Arbor.

That's where I met her. I was just 16. This would have been around 1981. She was like some alien creature, so radiant and beautiful but in an ugly, deranged sort of way, I don't know if you noticed. Even decades later. She never lost that radiance. She looked like a model who'd fallen down the stairs one too many times. Her elbows were bulgy and she had this awkward, crane-like way of walking.

But everything came together when she picked up a guitar. I was designing anti- protectorate flyers and sometimes I'd go to Second Chance or the Blind Pig just to see some random band. I'd never heard of Psycho Femmes. Patti and I became instant friends even though I don't have an ounce of musical talent and even though Patti always denies she has any talent she's really a very skilled musician.

I thought there should be a *the*. THE Psycho Femmes.

But Patti said it was in line with Talking Heads and, later, Ghost in Machine and that the THE would put the emphasis on singularity, while just Psycho Femmes was for all women not just the band. Patti was the first one who ever talked openly to me about politics, not local politics but national, which of course meant talking about the protectorate, something I'd never done before. I don't know how it was with you Antony but none of my friends talked about such things. We didn't need to be told not to talk politics, I think we'd internalized the fear. I guess that's the way very subtle social engineering and propaganda work: if it's done well enough it doesn't need to be enforced.

Psycho Femmes, God! All their songs were in the future tense. As if everything great or terrible was yet to happen. As if we hadn't seen anything yet. You know how punk was supposed to be all about NO FUTURE? Well, the Femmes embraced that blankness and wrote themselves, their own fantasies, into it. If the future really was a void then why not fill it with something? The band was guitars only even though all the rage at that time was synthesizers. It was Patti on Stratocaster (of course!) and then a bunch of different girls rotating through on Schecter Hellraisers and Chapman Baritones that Patti's brother had stolen. If punk was the same three chords fast and loud then Psycho Femmes was three chords slow and louder.

I came away from their shows turning lyrics over in my head that I'd sworn I'd heard but of course there was no singer in the band and no lyrics to be sung. And yet there they were: words to songs I hadn't heard. This was the band's secret power and I'm sure I'm not the only one who discovered a hidden part of themselves during those shows. Oh I know this sounds absurd Antony and I'm not even sure how to say it and maybe there is no way to say it. All I mean is that without Psycho Femmes lyrics like "She is on a journey / during the night / the end of which keeps receding" (which they never sang!) I wouldn't have changed like I did, changed into someone open to the idea of rebelling. You only know a part of me Antony, a very small part.

I can't tell you now—especially in a letter like this under these circumstances—what I had to endure to become the person I was in Detroit. All I can say here is that it's not in my nature to rebel. It was so hard for me to become strong enough to resist—to openly and defiantly resist—the protectorate. If we're lucky, Antony, someday I can see you again and we can tell each other our stories.

OUR SETS ARE AS SHORT AS OUR SKIRTS.

That was the Psycho Femmes slogan for a while.

It's funny how in life under the protectorate we embraced all the old binaries we'd worked so long to free ourselves from. Wearing short skirts used to be ironic, a way to distance ourselves from our mothers. But then somehow it became important again for us to, I don't know, re-assert the old codes that'd gotten us this far. And the fact that Patti was capable of off-stage violence, that meant a lot to us. We trusted and feared her. I saw it myself one day when I was late for a planning meeting and I went to her apartment. She lived near the Ambassador Bridge, near Corktown, in one of those old brick buildings from the 1920s. The sound of cars going over the bridge sounded like some sort of permanent military assault. I was about to knock on her door but I heard something that stopped me.

A voice from inside, a muffled voice, pleading, begging. I listened until I couldn't bear it any longer and when I saw Patti later I didn't ask her about it but I noticed the scratches on her arms and the dried blood beneath her nails and I knew what she had done, but not why, or to whom. To be honest Patti would have been a good torturer for the protectorate and that's one of the complicating things, isn't it, that there are good and bad people on both sides? I don't think she's ever killed anybody but I've seen her hurt people.

One time I found her crying in the dark—this was when we lived in Ann Arbor—just sitting in a chair in the dark crying. She must have heard me come in because she stopped, but then started again. I went to turn on the light but she said *don't*. So, I stood there while she cried, the only light coming in from the moon and the refrigerator kicked on which broke the tension a little. I knew then that she had done something terrible, something really terrible Antony, maybe for the first time.

I was jealous, actually.

I've never been able to cry. Antony, it's true. The only time I can remember is when I was stung by a wasp. I've tried to cry which is ridiculous. I've watched sad movies on purpose and I've imagined people I love suffering or dying but I'm dry-eyed throughout it all.

One of the things Patti did with Psycho Femmes was put out a fanzine, Xeroxed and stapled. Of course, everyone we knew was doing the same thing but that was part of the fun, the spirit of it all, and for some weird reason for a short while there was a collective rush among all the bands to see who could come up with the most homey, domestic fanzine. I can't explain why, but there was this enormous desire to replicate what we thought our grandmothers had done and we were completely unironic about it: sewing, baking, tending to small gardens. It wasn't nostalgia but something deeper, a sort of love for an imagined way of being.

For Patti's Psycho Femmes fanzine she included these recipes she'd collected from fans, really elaborate recipes and then she'd a write a little story or anecdote about them. There was one, I remember, that involved chicken cooked on an iron skillet with spices and seasonings I'd never heard of and a story she wrote about how it was served in a park on a picnic table with the sun coming through the trees and a cool breeze off the river. There was another one involving some sort of custard pie, an even longer recipe and story that probably took up half the fanzine. This one was served—in the story—at a restaurant that had just reopened after a fire, and everything tasted of smoke or customers thought so because the idea of the fire was still fresh in their minds.

In the story, the custard pie was the only item on the menu that didn't taste or smell of smoke and after a few months the only thing the restaurant served was custard pies.

It's silly, isn't it, and yet I remember it so well. We shared a tiny apartment with soft wooden floors for a while and Patti would labor at night on the zine, in between writing new songs, at the small kitchen table where she had her typewriter, glue, razors, and a black ink marker. She'd design the pages in light pencil, marking out boxes where the text would go and then she'd type the recipes and stories and gossip and a horoscope right into those boxes.

Sometimes she'd ask me for help, to proofread or to come up with horoscopes or to staple them together after she'd made copies at the library. The way the copiers worked was that you'd check out a cartridge counter at the circulation desk and slot it into the machine and it would keep track of how many copies you made.

Then when you'd turn it back in they'd read the number and you'd pay for that number of pages. But one time something went wrong with the cartridge and it stopped counting at around 20 or 25 copies so we just kept going and made as many as we could. I think for that issue we made over a 100 zines when normally we'd make about half that.

That was the year that the protectorate decided to ration electricity. What a disaster that was, do you remember? It was during the summer, nighttime into early morning, from 11:30 to 4:00 am or something and I remember how much we laughed at the seeming randomness of that. Why 11:30? Why not 11:00 or midnight? We found it so funny and clumsy. 11:30! That just gave us so much hope that the protectorate was doomed, somehow.

Of course, a black market for electricity sprung up almost overnight and plus it was so easy to get around the meters they installed by ███ and disconnecting the black wire every night at 11:30 and then re-attaching it in the morning. But before people began to figure out how to do that there was a certain beauty, a certain stillness, to the city at night, absent of so much artificial light. I'd sometimes take to walking at night, at first just short strolls to the park not far from our apartment but then longer ones out to the edges of Ann Arbor, just soaking up the dark. The air felt different, cleaner, though I know of course it wasn't.

There was a spot down at the Huron River, an old wooden dock, and that's where I found the bag of money—did I mention the money before or did Patti?—it was on one of those nighttime walks. There was a dilapidated, tornado-damaged house with its aluminum siding blown off on the river that had been for sale for a long time and no one was there and there was a path through the side yard, down a hill, to the river. I'd go there on occasion just to sit and listen to the frogs and look at the sky and one time there was a burlap bag on the end of the dock, like it had been tossed up there from a passing boat.

That's still my theory of how it got there.

That it was some sort of clandestine drop-off and the person who was supposed to pick it up either hadn't gotten there yet or there was some sort of mix-up.

The weird thing is I just picked it up and started walking back to the apartment without even looking inside.

Something told me not to look, I don't know why, as if there was something cosmically dangerous about looking in that bag in the dark night.

So I just walked with it as if it had always been my bag.

Of course I didn't know what was inside but I knew it wasn't human parts.

I know that sounds terrible but my first thought was that it was parts of a person! When I got back Patti was sleeping. I emptied the bag on the couch and it was bundles of cash in rubber bands, just like in a movie. About ten thousand dollars. I decided right then to split it with Patti. I don't know why, it just seemed the right thing to do. For a long time after that—it continues to this day, really—I was paranoid that whosever money it was would come looking for it and eventually make their way to me, and I even slept with a carving knife under my pillow. Then after I met Paul I loaned him three thousand to help get the metal out of his back and the rest has gone to various projects against the protectorate.

One thing more about the Psycho Femmes. Patti used to plunge the stage into darkness for the first few songs and then the lights would come up slowly. It was quite dramatic and it helped to get the audience on their side early on. But one night—actually this was like the second or third time I'd seen them perform—one night at a place called The Heidelberg, as the lights came up there was a box on the stage, a box that clearly surprised the band. It was about the size of a really big suitcase, but clear. Transparent. It was hard to see what was inside because of the lights, the reflection. The glare. This was in Ann Arbor during that wave of micro bombings—do you know about those?—that terrorized the city that hot summer. Of course, everyone's mind rushed to give meaning to the box: it was a bomb, most likely, that an audience member had slipped onto the stage while it was dark, and it was up to Patti, as leader of Psycho Femmes, to deal with it.

Or it was a prank.

Or the band had placed it there themselves.

No matter, it was there at the foot of the stage, sucking in our thoughts. Into its thick glass. Was it glass? I don't know for sure. A few people in the audience left, and a few hurled beer bottles and even underwear at the box. Some people spat on it. Psycho Femmes was into these long, dark, metal songs at that time and she, Patti, stripped off her leather jacket and laid it over the box and I thought it was a gesture like you might do if you came across a fresh road kill, a small deer or a cat, how you might, if you were of a certain sensitivity, cover it with something out of respect for a little life lost. Patti's gesture had the strange effect of both acknowledging the box and disavowing it, as if to say, *yes, we see that you're here, now we're going to ignore you and play the fuck on!* And from that moment forward the audience ignored the box that might have held a bomb, or nothing of the kind, and so did the band. It seems like a nice story, right?

Well, the show ended with Psycho Femmes playing a cover of 'November 22 1963' by Destroy all Monsters, which they always did, and by 2:30 or 3:00 am everyone had left. The glass box had been tossed into the garbage in the alley and there it remained for two days until garbage was collected. *En route* to the city dump the truck exploded like a grenade whose shrapnel was garbage, killing the driver and the passenger of a car next to the truck. We didn't learn until much later that the garbage truck driver was Carlos Weir, one of the founders of the insurgency.

His face shredded up by the splintering glass.

They said they found a few of his teeth a block away, embedded in a telephone pole. A host of theories emerged: that he was the original target all along, or that Psycho Femmes themselves were somehow involved, or that it was all much simpler than that (in the way that truth is stranger than fiction) and that the bomb was meant to go off right there on the stage but that somehow its fuse had temporarily failed and that the box was carelessly tossed out and it was just coincidence that it killed Carlos.

No matter, Psycho Femmes were never the same. A cloud of doubt and suspicion hung over them. When, after a few months, it became clear that wherever they went and whatever music they made they'd always be associated with the murder of Carlos Weir, Patti disbanded them, although they still continued to make music on and off for the next several years.

They'd release singles with no cover art, no song titles, no names, just candy red vinyl 45s that would appear in paper-white sleeves in record stores without ceremony. I had a friend who lived in Fresno during that time and she said that the records would even show up there, in out-of-the-way record stores. Even though I'm close with Patti I still don't know how they disseminated those red, covert Psycho Femmes singles all across the country. You could tell the songs were recorded fast, faster even than a lot of lo-fi punk music at the time. Patti never even told me about it.

She'd just disappear for a few days and come back and then several weeks later the records would appear. It became like a game between us never to mention it. I know I wanted to ask her about it and I sensed she wanted to tell me but neither one of us ever brought it up and I think I know why: we were both practicing deceit. Deceit in service of some larger cause, in this case the insurgency. We deceived each other with our feigned ignorance. I knew that Patti knew that I knew that Psycho Femmes were behind those records. And maybe the glass box. And maybe the death of Carlos Weir. And Patti knew that I knew that she knew this. Added to that the complication that we both happened to be seeing and sleeping with the same guy (although he didn't know that we knew this) and it made for a tense year plagued with intrigue.

This was one of Paul's friends and in fact it was the guy who got him into pinball machines. His name was Rico.

Well, Frederick but everyone called him Rico. He was dashing.

Very old-fashioned.

He had this thing where he'd adjust his horn-rimmed glasses with one hand, with his middle finger and thumb. There was something also stately about it—it's hard to say why. He had all these little gestures like that. He sometimes had a cigarette behind his ear but I never saw him smoke. He came from a divided family: his mother had been a muckety-muck in the protectorate and his father a pamphleteer for the insurgency and so of course we could never trust him. He said he was neutral but we—Patti especially—never trusted anyone neutral. You were either for the protectorate or against it. God, she's so binary. But we never talked about any of that. Not with Rico. This was one of Patti's hang-ups, not to mix sex and politics, which is impossible, right?

I guess if you psychoanalyzed her you'd say she had intimacy problems, but what does that mean?

That she likes to fuck without getting close.

It's all just so much patriarchal bullshit anyway. All the 'great minds' of psychiatry are men, right, at least until recently. Have you ever read Freud's Dora case? The mute hysteric! Patti was obsessed with it for a while and that's actually where she got the idea for the name Psycho Femmes.

All of which is to say, Antony, that I've included a cassette. It's not labeled but I think it's from the show with the box. I want you to hear it.

Maybe they're not treating you as bad as I fear they are and they'll let you listen, and if you listen closely you can hear the hum of the box. I hadn't noticed it at the time but listening to the tape there it is, like a siren or a wail just beneath the noise of the band and the crowd.

When I listen to it now I imagine it's a signal. A warning.

Rachel

October 19, 1999

Dear Antony,

Have you listened to the tape I wonder? I listened to it again
and imagined you were as well at the same time. Could you
hear the hum of the box?

Do you know what babies do at three weeks? Sleep.

At least girl babies do. Maybe boy ones too. Maybe all
babies. I worry that they sleep too much but Julia says that's
what they do. What's it like to sleep as a baby? Do they
dream? What is there to dream about?

Even though they're twins they don't look alike. Will they
grow to look alike? The truth is they don't look like anything
or anyone, not me or you or anybody. They just look like
babies. They smell just like you'd think babies would. They
are almost cliché babies.

You weren't the first to come in here, you know. There
had been others. Did Charlotte tell you that? Did she?
Probably not. This location and what we're up to is hardly
a secret to those who want to restore the protectorate, so
we're pretty vigilant, although I must say it took us a few
hours to peg you. The last one they sent to Detroit, her
cover story was far less believable and anyway she tipped
her hand early, finding her way around far too easily for
someone who'd *never been* to Detroit before. You should
have seen what Paul did to her hands. But Paul was different
back then. He'd do things like that to people. Paul said he
knew right away and you didn't fool him but then he's a big
talker and was always trying to impress me and Julia. He
had the basement at Fletcher's to take care of and he was
obsessed with that. Keeping it clean for ▮▮▮ . I hope you

never become familiar with that basement. Even where you are now, Antony, can't be as bad.

We couldn't count on Julia to sniff out interlopers like you. She had no antennae or feel for deception. Her generation never developed that ironic edge, that edge that distances you just enough from what's happening around you. Her scars were real. Did I tell you that already? I think I did. I can't remember. Although that nonsense story about how she got them during a growth spurt is hers. With people like you coming around, you can see why she couldn't tell anyone how she really got them, at the hands of the protectorate.

"The protectorate!" Like it's some abstraction. Which is the problem, isn't it. "The protectorate did this" or "the protectorate did that" or "thanks to the protectorate." Like it wasn't real people with real intentions and real hands and knives and real blood and bones.

Blood is real, right?

Broken fingers and faces, nothing fake about that.

Acid poured down your throat, or between your legs if you're a woman. That's about as real as it gets.

People censor themselves without even knowing it. You knew right where to find that church, didn't you? It was almost sweet how you let Paul mark those danger points on the map, as if you didn't know. We'd actually gotten word from ███ that someone like you'd be coming, so it wasn't a total surprise and since we knew you already knew something about how the drone sabotagery worked, we ouldn't very well hide it. We had to carry on with at least some normalcy, although of course parts of it were a ruse. I actually had a dream about you last night—right after I'd fallen back to sleep after feeding the girls—except that the dream wasn't about you directly. So I guess it wasn't a dream about you but about something that reminded me of you.

I was sitting on a high cliff overlooking a vast desert and a sandstorm was moving, churning very slowly down below. It was completely silent and terrifying because there was a line of camels or men on camels very small, like brown ants, and the storm was approaching but I couldn't tell if they saw it or not, and I couldn't warn them. Beneath the storm was a black cloud, so the sand must have been in the air, travelling above the desert. I turned around to tell you Antony but you weren't there. I don't know why you would have been or why I should have expected you there.

It was just me on the cliff and it was the loneliest, saddest feeling.

So real that when I woke up I thought I'd find sand in my bed but of course I didn't. Things like that never happen.

The packs of dogs you encountered, of course, were for real. I've never been menaced by them but they make the news every once in awhile so people get this idea that they're vicious. Paul was a different story though and to hear him tell it, dogs are no better than bugs or vermin. He had no liking for them whatsoever. One time they got into the storeroom and destroyed a bunch of freshly painted red drone parts while hunting for food and he tracked them down with a shotgun he kept behind the bar. He went out into the streets like a vigilante looking for dogs with red paint on them. He brought them back to the basement and I don't want to know what he did to them. Paul's owned this place since Grandy, who was a poet and publisher during the Black Arts movement. He first published Gwendolyn Brooks and Dudley Randall and, I think, Rita Dove and Philip Levine, if I remember correctly.

They say Grandy was named after Grand Boulevard, which is where the Grande Ballroom is. But you should know that from your research. Some say that's where punk was first performed. Not at CBGB but at the Grande Ballroom, when MC5 live-recorded *Kick out the Jams* there in '68. So after Grandy died this place sat abandoned for the longest time, and then Paul bought it after the protectorate fell and it became the meeting place for those of us who believed that the battle against the protectorate wasn't yet over but had just entered a different, more covert phase.

And we turned out to be right, didn't we? People like you kept showing up and proving it. It was Paul who reached out to me. I was working at the Arts Institute—that's when they were restoring the Rivera murals—and he came in. I was a student docent and he was in one of the groups and he slipped me an envelope with a key in it (Paul and his keys!) and an address for a locker at a gym on the north side. Inside the locker was another with some photocopied documents. They were some of my mother's reports as an informer for the protectorate, observations about people whose names I didn't know but who may have suffered terribly because of them.

When I say mother I mean it in the mothering sense. The woman who raised me. I don't know the name of my birth mother nor, as far as I can tell, does anybody. That's what happened to the women who raised protectorate orphans like me, right Antony? But don't tell that to our ▆▆ because ▆▆ know how much he hates any truths that contradict his. I can't say that I was abandoned because that suggests intent and for all I know something happened to the woman who gave birth to me, something she did not intend to happen.

They were so banal, "mother's" remarks, who-said-what about what characters at the book clubs and I remember one in particular. *Jane Eyre* was the book and the line was: "I have an inward treasure born with me, which can keep me alive if all outward delights should be withheld." Are you surprised I know it by heart? I've already been reciting it to the girls. I know so many lines from that book by heart. My mother, however, used that line as evidence against one of the women in the reading group. It's hard to say how I intuited all this but if you had seen the report you'd understand. Do you understand, Antony?

Wait. Don't answer.

Or wait. Answer later, at the end.

If we ever meet face to face again Antony you can answer me then.

I was in Detroit during the protectorate's final crackdown. I was there at the Wayne State riots and was in the cafeteria when the helicopter came down. I hid out in the undergrad library for a few days, in the stacks.

And that's where I first read Hegel. God.

I was holed up in the philosophy section, of all places.

So, I passed my time with Hegel and honestly I thought a lot about what he had to say about freedom. Objective freedom and subjective freedom. It's hard to understand and I haven't read enough Kant, whom he quotes all over the place, but you really need time alone and in the quiet to get Hegel, I think. *An individual's interests and the interests of the state or government need to be aligned.* Really? Anyway, I spent a lot of time with Hegel and I feel like it helped me. I came close to being caught once when a ▓▓▓ came through. It was by chance, really, that they didn't see me. They must have been a lazy patrol because they turned around and left before they got to my row. That's what radicalized me, though I don't like that word because why should being human and decent be considered 'radical?' Seeing and, worse than that, hearing those students being gunned down—seeing it in real life not just hearing rumors about it—made me remember how I used to feel when I was a girl, when every little thing meant so much to me. I'd cry at the death of a fucking beetle.

Even things like marbles and fireflies, and hearing those students die made something well up inside and overflow and I felt like I was a girl again. It was as if years of accumulated cynicism had evaporated and I decided that if there was anything I could do, no matter how small, to hasten the end of the protectorate I'd do it, so that's how I got into the drone business, as they say. What you saw here was just part of an enormous network.

You were nowhere near to figuring it out Antony. You didn't even come close.

Rachel

Antony

RACHEL, JULIA, AND I HEADED BACK DOWN LIVERNOIS towards the warehouse. Except this time it was a sunny, breezy, warm afternoon, any mood of menace or danger dispelled by the leaves moving in the trees lining the street and the sound of birds and locusts and a distant train with its mournful horn. I just remember that so well. I've been told it's important to try to remember things like that, the little in between moments, not just the big stuff.

Julia carried the duffel bag slung over her shoulder.

The streets were wet although there was no indication it had rained. I remember these things and not because I listened to the tapes:

The sweet, rotten smell of old coffee.

The exposed patches of brick beneath the asphalt.

The bold fat raccoon that shouldn't be there in the daylight.

The faded yellow plastic Superman kite tangled in the power lines.

Julia carried the duffel bag, slung over her shoulder like empty skin. The street lights flashed red but no one obeyed them, the occasional car barreling through intersections.

"What'd the guys in the car say?" Julia asked.

We turned left at an unmarked intersection, following the same route Rachel and I had taken on our first errand to deliver the keys to the warehouse.

"They said, one of them said, that Paul Fletcher had taken over from Grandy and that he was Top Dog and caused a lot of damage in his day," I said.

"Is that all?"

"And that I was to deliver a message to him."

"Which was?"

"That Chu Chu remembers," I said.

Julia laughed. The small teardrop tattoos beneath her eye seemed to activate somehow in the sun, and they were beautiful.

We passed the apartment building where the woman, the last time we walked here, had glowered at me from an upper window, and now, in the daylight I could see that same window, with red drapes drawn across it, red drapes that reminded me of an inferno or a gateway into an inferno and if they had parted ever so slightly to reveal that face I wouldn't have been surprised, in fact I half-expected it, the face of the woman who had looked at me accusingly but who was absent now, as if by her absence she was condemning me. Although it probably hadn't been more than a glance or furtive look up at that apartment window, it feels now like I had stared at it for hours, observing every detail of the red fabric hung as a curtain undulating in the open window like ocean swells in slow motion or billows of thick smoke.

"So who's Chu Chu?" I asked.

It was Rachel who answered. "Not who but what."

I caught a sudden whiff of garlic from a hole-in-the wall Korean take-out place.

They had a grimy, greasy-yellow box fan set up in the open doorway as if to exhaust the smells from the night. An old, wrinkled man in white overalls sat outside the door on a fold- out chair with wooden slats.

"It's going to sound crazy, unless you're from around here, but Chu Chu was a tree," Julia said.

"A tree," I said.

"A famous old tree, a Shingle Oak, nicknamed Chu Chu. Who knows why, some say because of the nearby rail yards, the tree a native survivor from the logging days, a reminder of the era before Cadillac and his horde French rapists and murderers arrived. Chu Chu stood at a hidden location at the eastern edge of the city. Then one day it was damaged beyond saving, its bark hacked into and poison poured over its exposed roots. It took years to die, which was even worse. Paul was arrested and charged with vandalizing Chu Chu and paid a fine, but his real punishment came at the hands of a radical eco group who ambushed him one night after he closed up and branded him. A circle with an X inside, burned into his back. So you see, he's scarred like the rest of us."

The warehouse loomed in the distance.

Julia handed the duffel bag to Rachel and then Rachel passed it to me like a game of hot potato with a danger- ous object, a dangerous object disguised as something very simple and obvious and harmless. I slung it over my shoul- der and, of course, imagined that I could feel the red pro- peller glowing, through the fabric, like a hot coal against my back. No, worse: like a probe that was reading my vital signs. A swarm of drones floated across the sky as they so often did, in a tight V formation as Canada geese do and I wondered when it happened that things like this no longer seemed shocking or unusual, like when TV was invented and it seemed impossible that images and sound could enter your house through a thin electrical cord but after a few seasons it all seemed routine.

I knew then, as Rachel, Julia, and I closed in on the blank warehouse, that I shouldn't go back to Fletcher's, that it was too dangerous for me there, that the Paul-person had somehow known about me from the beginning, my political sentiments, for I, as well, had marked him as a hold-out from the old protectorate, the protectorate *Tomorrows* had so ruthlessly satirized.

If you knew about Paul Fletcher you'd know about the damage, the guy in the car had said. Thinking back on it, I wonder if he meant the damage to the tree, Chu Chu, or damage of a different, more human sort? I'm trying to remember what Paul's first words to me were, but I can't, maybe something about smoking, that was it, something about how smoking was no longer permitted, something innocuous, and yet even in that there was a veiled threat, or at the least a statement with an edge to it, there was also a finality, as if he was pronouncing a sentence or a verdict, a declarative that ruled out all possible other meanings.

If he had destroyed the tree—a defenseless tree—then what other innocents had he cut down, I wondered, as we paused in the shadow of the warehouse which loomed like a brick fortress, taking up a half-dozen or so blocks, so expansive that your eyes couldn't take it all in and if I'm committed to telling the truth about what happened no matter how absurd or embarrassing, I'll say that the warehouse held some electric charge for me, and maybe for Rachel and Julia, too. Architecture can be sensual, it's true, but I'd never felt the force of this so strongly as that moment with

Julia and Rachel as we stood outside the warehouse walls, a warehouse whose inviting bricks may as well have been baked with the soaked blood of the Mound Builders who were there one thousand years before Christ and before that even . . . into deep time untold.

From an alley or small street carved between two warehouse structures a person emerged, and then another, a man and a woman, or a boy and a girl and it seemed obvious even to someone who had no skin in the game that they were coming for us, and for the duffel bag, which I was now holding. Without any warning Rachel took my hand, and it was so small yet firm and I could imagine it on the back of my neck as she gently pulled me forward to kiss her. I had grown attached to the sewn-in red drone propeller if only as a means of keeping myself active in the unfolding situation. It was Julia who said *Don't hand over the bag until they offer something in exchange*, as if this was some part of a negotiation ritual that she been through a hundred times before, and then Rachel chimed in, *bartering's the only language they know*.

A cloud passed over the sun and in the shade the enormous warehouse took on a different hue. The approaching couple, who looked to be maybe in their late teens, each wore a shirt that read, in bold black letters, PURPLE GANG, with a pixelated black-and- white photograph of a dead man in an expensive looking suit from an earlier era on a floor, face down. The only color was from a gunshot wound to the back of his neck, seeping out red.

"The Collingwood Manor Massacre," said Rachel.

"I thought that happened in Chicago," I said.

Rachel said that the three gunned-down guys were from Chicago gangland but the killings took place in Detroit, on Collingwood, about two miles away.

I think they were brother and sister, the couple we were meeting, or relatives, for they both had similar, feral-like close-set eyes and narrow noses.

Rachel told me later they were twins. They looked like foxes.

The girl kept almost snapping her fingers like some habit or tic.

She'd move her fingers like she was going to snap them, or snap them without making the snapping sound. She'd do it with her right hand, while she was walking, the hand to her side but making that movement with her middle finger and thumb. The boy wore a big silver chain and black leather combat boots with red laces and I imagined him as someone who hired himself out for violence, although that was just an impression. The brief conversation we had with them wasn't so much of a conversation as an exchange of phrases, and not for the first time l felt I was witnessing something rehearsed as if those involved were delivering scripted lines.

The girl started first, asking outright for the duffel bag, although there was no real heart of conviction in her request, to which Julia replied something like, *It's not going to be that easy.* The girl turned toward the boy and whispered something in his ear and he slipped off his small backpack and unzipped it, fishing around for something, that something being a folded sealed manila envelope. He passed it over to Julia who held it up to the sky as if to try to see what was inside, then she set it down on the sidewalk and gently opened it, revealing exactly what we were carrying in our duffel bag, except green, not red. A green drone propeller, about four inches long. Julia passed it over to Rachel, who examined it and then nodded to me approvingly, which I took to be my signal to pass the duffel bag over to the couple.

They immediately unzipped it, turned it inside out, and, with a pocket knife cut the red propeller out from its pocket. The boy seemed satisfied and he handed it to the girl who also looked at it closely, rubbing her fingers gently over it. She then took out an empty envelope from the boy's backpack, carefully placed the red propeller inside, and zipped it up. And with that they turned and walked away, heading back towards the warehouse.

It all happened much more quickly and with less drama than, frankly, I had hoped. Julia had told them it wasn't going to be easy, but it *was* easy, at least that's how it seemed to me. The sun had re-emerged from behind the clouds and for the first time I noticed an enormous antenna or antenna-like structure atop the warehouse, casting a shadow down the entire length of the street. The angle of the sun must have been just perfect, because the shadow bisected the street. Atop the antenna was a symbol, its shadow cast right there on the street before us: a circle with an X inside. The same symbol that, according to Rachel, was branded onto Paul's back.

The sky. The earth. All that space in between.

We had left the shadow of the warehouse and seemed to be lost in our own thoughts. An unfamiliar part of the city, probably just a few blocks over from Livernois, but for me it might as well have been miles.

I remember this: a young woman riding a non-motorized wheelchair in a sequined denim cape came out of an apartment building from across the street, down a janked, makeshift plywood ramp, the palms of her hands riding just above the tops of the wheels in that familiar way, softly touching the wheels as they moved in order to slow herself down. At the bottom of the ramp she stopped herself, put her hand above her eyes as if in salute to block the sun, and saw us. She raised her hand, extending her index and little finger in a gesture that signaled devil horns, as I had always known them, although of course it had outstripped that original meaning so who knows. Julia waved her over and without even having to look both ways she scooted across the street at a pretty good clip.

Her hair was so brightly red and she wore a faded jean jacket with punk or punk-era buttons. In a freak of coincidence, I recognized The Necros, from Maumee, Ohio, a little town south of Toledo on the Maumee River, a terrifying town only approachable, in the imagination, on a burning raft, a burning raft at night to illuminate its treacherous shores, either a burning raft or a raft with all its torches lit, gliding gently and stealthily across muddy waters. Those punk buttons. I noticed the safety pin, a small, pink safety pin, in her earlobe and I almost expected her to stand up from her wheelchair, like some Lazarus or Jesus and come striding over to me. And, in fact, she did stand from her chair to hug Julia and then Rachel.

"This is Antony," Julia said, "and this is Patti," and she hugged me. We were now four.

"Patricia Campbell Hearst, but they call me Patti," Patti said.

Patti's eyebrows were black and thick against the shock of her red hair.

The four of us: a greater number against the dogs and packs of dogs, homeless dogs that no one took a census of or counted in a serious and consistent way, in the way that the bodies of the missing during the protectorate's final years weren't counted, as if the arithmetic of bodies had become forbidden. I had no illusions about what I was up against, heading back to the bartender Paul, and we made our way down from Muirland towards McNichols, the sun like an anvil, and then it happened: Patti was not only up and out of her wheelchair but walking like an ace.

"You really going to see Yama tonight at the Old Miami?" Rachel asked.

"Shouldn't I?"

"Of course not," said Patti, the safety pin in her ear catching the sun and throwing off what looked like a spark. Her voice reminded me of something, of what I couldn't say, maybe a voice from a movie, maybe Nancy Allen's voice from *Dressed to Kill*, a Yonkers accent, or what I imagined a Yonkers accent to be (*wise guy, huh?*), a tough but dreamy thing, an impossible combination. Patti went on to say that Yama was of the devils, or associated with devils, and that they were a heavy metal band *in name only* and that their real reason for being was to recruit people at their shows, people who they could train in how to undermine and sabotage Detroit's so-called renaissance. What she was saying was so absurd that I looked to Rachel and then to Julia for some kind of reaction, like a laugh or a gesture or a look that said, *Oh, Patti and her stories*, but no, Rachel and Julia just stared straight ahead as we all walked together and I had to decipher Patti's comments on my own.

In the sunlight Patti's red hair glowed and I thought of the red suckers I used to love as a kid, Dum Dum's from the barbershop jar (the barber: he also happened to be the butcher in our town and a known seducer of young girls) and I wondered if Patti had ever tried to hide from someone in a large crowd but had been unsuccessful because her hair was like a red siren calling her out. She said that one of Yama's band members—whom no one could identify because he never performed with the band on stage—was always planted in the audience to scout and recruit those who would work to derail and sabotage Detroit's progress, either through strategic vandalism, computer hacking, rumor mongering, or other, more provocative means. I nearly laughed out loud but Patti was telling me this with such casual conviction and in the context of all the other strange things that had happened to me over the past 40 or so hours, a part of me believed her.

"In fact, there's some of their handiwork right there, I suspect," and she pointed to a billboard across the street that had been defaced with black paint to read "Hitsville U.S.A." except that instead of the Motown record logo there was a black fist. *You probably don't believe me but it's not my job to convince you*, she said and the light in her hair was so strong and that's when I noticed she had this thing, she'd do this thing where she'd tap her thigh with the palm of her hand, and then bring her hand up to her chest where she'd put it over her heart. The whole process only lasted a second or two but it was weirdly endearing and I felt, somehow, that it revealed more about Patti than anything she could ever say.

We stopped at a Lafayette Coney food cart and each got something and then crossed the street to a playground and sat on benches to eat. Julia kicked off her shoes and then so did Rachel, an old pair of red Converse high tops and Rachel had bandages wrapped around both feet. She saw me looking and said, *They tried to crucify me.* Patti laughed but Julia scowled and said *Come on, Patti, you know better than that* and then she asked me why I hadn't taken my shoes off and I said I preferred to keep them on, especially when eating.

What she didn't tell you, Julia said to me, glancing over at Patti, *is that she had a history with Yama*, and it wasn't a good one.

Then she went on to explain how Patti (and Patti just sat there scarfing her hotdog and didn't interrupt or correct Julia) had been recruited by the band when she was just 15 and had been passed around from member to member as a sexual toy and that this had given her access to some very sensitive information, information that she didn't know what to do with when she was 15 but that when she got older realized was very shocking and damaging. The gist of it was that the band didn't hide from Patti their deep and extensive efforts *to keep Detroit destroyed*, as they said, maybe because they thought she was only 15 and *just a girl*, but for whatever reason Patti was around during some of the meetings where they plotted vandalism and crimes, such as the explosion that brought down the Woodward water tower in '93 (still unsolved) and other things, *some twisted shit that I'll bet she'd rather I not tell you about, that right Patti?* Julia asked Patti, who quietly listened to these stories about herself with a blank or neutral expression on her face. And a sadness.

"No need to tell him everything," Patti finally said, speaking about me as if I wasn't there, even though I was sitting just a few feet from her.

"Yeah, he's not a trustworthy sort, according to Paul," said Rachel.

Of course, *Beyond Blue Tomorrows* was there in the blank back horizon of my mind, like a distant black cloud that kept deforming and reforming. I could feel myself getting closer to it as if I had somehow entered its orbit. In the Detroit sky above us, three vultures keeled in that circular way of theirs and I wondered if what I'd read was true, that they'd made drones now disguised as birds, although everything was out in the open now so I'm not sure why anyone would want to disguise them.

I didn't know what to make of Julia's story about Patti's abuse at the hands of Yama, and walking next to her, headed vaguely in the direction of Fletcher's, I wondered, as I inevitably did when walking next to a woman, what it would be like to hold her hand. What a stupid, primitive thought, and yet I felt you could detect a lot by holding the hand of someone you don't know very well. It's an awkward act. All the secret codes involved in who's going to let go first, the sweaty palms, fingers interlocked or more like a handshake. It's strangely intimate, parts of your bodies touching out in the open and yet so much ambiguity about the meaning of it all.

"Of the devils, how?" I asked Patti. We had crossed Muirland and were walking east on Grove and I could see the university's art deco clock tower in the distance. There were, I'd been told, a family of falcons that roosted up there and I thought I could hear their piercing cries, such a mournful sound.

A car in a driveway backfired and a bunch of kids rode by on high-handlebarred bikes.

A blue garbage truck slowly backed out of an alley, its back-up beeper going. The streets smelled of sweet refuse.

In the distance a siren wailed, a child cried.

"Everything Julia said was true, if that's what you're asking," Patti said, "and there's more that's worse. Yama are a bunch of demonic fucking psychopaths and if you go to that show at the Old Miami you're crazy. I'm not the only girl they ruined and if you're wondering how they keep getting away with it then you've got a lot to learn about the levels of corruption in this city."

It was the first time any of them had talked to me so directly and unambiguously and to be honest it felt like someone had thrown cold water in my face.

"And the part Julia told about them destroying Detroit, that's true too, and also worse than what she described." Rachel and Julia were walking some distance ahead of us now, and maybe that's why Patti suddenly opened up. "Of course they don't *call* it destruction, they call it deprogramming," she said. "They're hung up on names for things. And they're not the only ones. There's a cabal of Detroit bands—I don't know why it's bands mostly—that want to keep the city down and ungentrified and terrifying. Some are pretty mild, and some are more extreme, like Yama, who don't just front black metal but really believe it and live it and have gone in their minds into black areas you can't even imagine.

Detroit's known, to those who tune in to its black signals, as a place to come to for this sort of thing. You've probably never heard of the Witch of Delray. In the 1930s a lot of people who she came into contact with died, falling off ladders, alcohol poisoning. She was probably just a greedy person who killed a lot of men for their money but these rumors grew up around her about spells and black magic and she's a hero to bands like Yama, who titled their first album—Veres—after her."

"It's all too much," I said, not sure how else to put it.

We'd turned north on pot-holed Fairfield and were heading back toward McNichols and, presumably, Fletcher's, where towering Paul waited for us with who knew what sort of other nonsensical errands to run. But I'd had enough and was determined to say my goodbyes at the bar and disappear into the night alone for a while. The vultures still circled themselves against the blue, cloudless sky, and had now become five, rotating counterclockwise. A car wash was opening up, a man in a baggy Pistons tee shirt putting the painted sign out and another one hosing down the pavement that led into the wash.

A woman at a bus stop rearranged some object in her large purse.

The kids on the bikes rode by again and stopped to look at a wounded or dead cat at the side of the road.

I thought again about reaching over and taking Patti's hand.

I wondered how black metal, as Patti had described Yama, was different from the heavy metal of my youth which was all pretty hokey and harmless. And there was that tug again, that feeling that I was being drawn closer to *Beyond Blue Tomorrows* and into Evie's world. We headed north on Livernois at the McNichols intersection and in the distance I saw someone who appeared to be Paul attaching an American flag to a flagpole jutting from beside the awning.

"It's never a good sign when Paul puts the flag out," said Rachel.

It's hard to explain how I had come around to the Colonel's, the protectorate's, way of thinking. If I could say it was nothing more than just fashion, in the end, I would, but it was something else. It wasn't just that I'd come, under the Colonel's fatherhood and tutelage, to understand that power and power alone moved history forward, and that real power always belonged to those who controlled—although that's not the right word—who shaped—the very nature of language that gave rise to "dissent" or "insurgent voices" in the first place. On certain days, the Colonel's patched together aphorisms sometimes constituted his only words to me, phrases like *History and the unconscious are the last great myths*, or *No longer are the ruins of knowledge lamentable for the ruins themselves are defunct*, or *Information dissolves meaning.*

He'd work these over under his breath and then spring them on me as bold pronouncements.

After what happened to Doubting Thomas I began to read poetry, all of it that I could find, it didn't matter whether it was old or new or who wrote it, I just had a sudden and burning desire to consume as much of it as I could and it was here that I found my voice, or a reflection of my voice, in the ambiguous spaces between the lines and in the way some lines broke naturally and with meaning and some broke violently and suddenly and without reason. It was here that I recognized the leveraging power of those line breaks and felt a kind of cold thrill when a poem worked its wonder this way, freeing me from the feeling that I was *in trouble.*

Because during my childhood with the Colonel, *trouble* meant something very specific. I'd be sent to my room and in the night I'd hear the voices, lying on my floor, my ear to the heat vent, the basement door opening and shutting, the muted screams, the lights flickering, the abyss of silence that followed and trailed me into my sleep, my teenage brain struggling to fill in the gaps, to figure out what was happening in my home and who the Colonel, really, was, who he *really was* when he was not with me. His uniform disguised him, and yet I was old enough to understand that we all wore uniforms, we all wore masks, and that the only danger was in wearing a mask that disguised us from ourselves. Did my father know who he was? Did he have what they call insight? Did he know that even as a child I somehow knew that what I needed from him he was either unwilling or unable to give?

His green-starched uniform clarified something, made it very distinct and visible, but what? I hated its clarity, but then came to admire it, to admire it as a complex code that needed to be cracked. I knew, from a very young age, that the uniform symbolized those in power, but who were those in power? As the Colonel's son I was protected from the violence that visited the sons and daughters of parents who did not wear the uniform, such as Doubting Thomas. But what ideas were associated with those in power (the *protectorate*), I'd wondered, and soon came to understand that there was only one idea that mattered to those in power: the idea of power itself.

The Colonel liked to say that if the protectorate collapsed it would be because people had forgotten how to fear it: that fear needed memory to work. He considered it his job, his duty, I suppose, to remind people how to fear.

He taught me how to fear, and how to hate.

What I didn't tell you about my unfortunate friend Thomas was that I discovered years later than he hadn't been executed for his insurgent pamphlets at all, but quite the opposite: he'd been rewarded. The Colonel had planted him as my friend and used him to tease out and guide my inevitable political awakening. Better to have someone doing it from the inside than some random outsider, some *real* friend. When Thomas was "discovered," interrogated, and executed, I'd seen what lengths the protectorate, and the Colonel, were willing to go and, cowardly or eager-to-please son that I was, I toyed with the ideas of the insurgency for only a little self-satisfied while before understanding fully and completely that my duty, my destiny, was with the (now defunct) protectorate.

It was then, I must have been 15 or 16, that I began my training as an editor, which initially meant summarizing dissident and insurgent pamphlets for the protectorate, distilling their ideas and strategies into simple concepts for people like the Colonel. I remember reading somewhere how this was not uncommon among dictators of the past, how, for instance, Pinochet was fascinated by (perhaps attracted to) the Marxist ideas he despised so much and murdered so many people over, or how the Nazi leadership collected and proudly displayed in their own homes the "decadent" Jewish art they supposedly despised and couldn't bear to look at.

Four years later, by the time the protectorate had temporarily collapsed and the Colonel and so many like him had either committed suicide or fled into exile, I'd already insinuated myself as a mole into the insurgent movement, while still secretly working for what was left of the protectorate. In truth, we (the protectorate) had always known that Detroit was the epicenter of resistance, especially postcolonial collapse, where people like Paul and Rachel and the sisters would continue their doomed work to ensure the protectorate wouldn't re-gather itself and come back.

"Antony, grab the flag," Julia said as we entered Fletcher's. It was a simple design: a red circle against an orange background. As I grabbed the flag pole to remove it from the holder the feel of it reminded me of something: the pole from the greenhouse.

"Did the twins come through?" Paul asked, still hunched over *Temple of Doom*, staring at the backglass as if it held some inscrutable secret to Indy's survival.

"The twins *always* come through," Julia replied, fishing out the green drone propeller from her pocket and setting it on the bar. I of course understood—although Rachel, Julia, Patti, and Paul didn't know that I understood—that the green and red propellers were sabotaged, defective on purpose but in ways that weren't obviously visible. In a complex network of exchanges, part of which I was witnessing, the defective propellers would make their way onto the protectorate's (or what was left of the protectorate, its sub- groups and splinter groups) drones, rendering them unstable and difficult to use. The phone behind the bar began to ring and I knew exactly who it was but I played dumb and it was then, at that moment, that I began to waver, that the old sentimentality crept in which had always burdened me and kept me useless for the sort of violence that was expected of me. For I knew what my betrayal of these people I'd spent two days with would mean for them, for their minds, for their bodies. It was a brutal game, not that I had any illusions about what would happen to me if my true role was discovered, for even Rachel, I was sure, wouldn't hesitate to turn me over to the likes of giant Paul, men for whom calibrated slaughter had become a condition for their existence.

I was familiar with the logic, the logic that said that the trail of dead bodies he'd left behind would be meaningless, or rather that Paul's actions would be meaningless, unless he continued until the end, the very end, the terrible terminus of all his actions. To give meaning to the death of his pro-protectorate victims he had to continue killing, or else it was all for nothing.

As I sat there at the familiar table, with a beer brought over by Julia, I wondered if I'd unexpectedly tipped my hand in my telling of the story of how I'd stopped in front of that ruined church at the corner of Livernois and 7 Mile, the one Paul warned me about with the blue dot. It was Rachel who'd questioned me about the church, and when I lied and told her I hadn't gone inside, that I'd been interrupted by the guys in the car who gave me the Old Miami flyer, something in her eyes shifted, as if she knew what I was saying wasn't true, but in what sense it wasn't true she didn't know. For I had indeed gone into the church, that notorious space where the original insurgents—the ones who ultimately brought down the protectorate in 1978—met clandestinely and where a core group of them was betrayed, trapped, and murdered in 1976, setting back the final push against the protectorate by two years. Julia sat down across from me with her own beer while Paul still stared at the pinball machine as if it held some secret he was about to break. Rachel and Patti were up at the bar, laughing about something. The afternoon sun spilled in through the open door and it all seemed, at that moment, elaborately staged, like a set from a play. I imagined I was in another place, in another time.

Oh yes, I *had* entered the dilapidated church, running my hand along its fallen steeple, which reminded me of an enormous unicorn horn with tall weeds and saplings growing up around it. The sadness of great distances across the Great Plains of a childhood vacation. The gaping church doors awaited with weird intention. There's something about an abandoned church, maybe even for non-believers, that feels tugged at in all the wrong ways, as if the religion—whatever religion—had lost a battle against whatever dark forces it had set itself against. A church is such a stark symbol of one set of ideas arrayed against another.

In this case, the interior was remarkably intact except for the altar, which had been foully desecrated. The pews were mostly still there, albeit wounded by vandals and age, some coated in black spray paint, the stairs to the basement littered with paper bags and needles. The basement was lit with just enough light from a high window to reveal the battered metal chairs, the long tables. This was probably where it had happened, and apart from wires attached to walls and some stains on the floor you'd never know that a dozen or so insurgents were murdered here, most likely on the orders of the Colonel. As if she'd had momentary access to my thoughts Julia said, *It's a good thing you stayed away from the blue- dot areas.* She was already half-way through her beer, as if summoning courage.

"I was tempted to go inside, I'll admit," I said.

"Tempted by the church?"

"Don't churches and temptation go hand-in-hand?"

"Do they?" Julia asked, finishing her beer.

I felt she was on to me, maybe they were all on to me and Julia was the one designated to conduct this interrogation disguised as conversation.

Julia stood up and went behind the bar to pour herself another one. She'd said she was Nigerian. How true was that? I wondered.

Was she a deceiver too, like me?

A gust of summer wind came through the door. In blew some sand and an empty paper cup.

Paul had finally abandoned the *Temple of Doom* machine and was over examining the green propeller on the counter.

The phone started to ring again and again it was ignored by everyone.

Before Julia stepped out from behind the bar I caught her eye and signaled for another one and she drew me another beer, too. She sat down across from me at the table and took off her jacket. That design stitched across the back of that black jacket, the three circles each with a crooked X trapped inside, something that reminded me of the A breaking free of the circle in those old anarchist symbols.

The white tank top. Her arms. The thought of her arms. The gentle scars streaming down her neck which in this light looked wet, like fresh snail trails.

"I don't know," I said, "I always thought of churches as the least tempting places."

"Which means you didn't go inside?"

"Didn't I say I didn't go inside?"

"That is what you said. Just curious."

We sipped our beers and I thought about why Julia and I were on different sides. We seemed in tune, and yet she had thrown her lot in with witches and the insurgents and who knows what other forces of disorder, while I, even after escaping the terrible shadow of the Colonel, understood all too well the need for order and the authority to maintain that order. I must have been staring at the coin-like object in her hair because she fished it out from one of the dreads, rubbed it between her fingers, and dropped it on the table in front of me. It was like a coin except fatter, about the size of a flattened marble, with a small hole near the center that Julia had woven a few strands of hair through to hold it in place. I picked it up and felt it there the palm of my hand. Julia took it back and dropped it in her jacket pocket.

"There are all sorts of stories of people coming to Detroit looking for one thing and finding something else, something they hadn't expected," Julia said. "Isn't that right Rachel?"

Rachel gave the thumbs up sign from the bar without turning around. "You mean like wandering into a concert by a band like Yama?"

"Worse than that," Julia said, holding her beer up as if to examine it. "People think of Detroit as an Open City but that's just bullshit."

The thin scars on Julia's dark neck seemed illuminated somehow, as if lit by a powerful light inside her body that was barely visible in these weak, thin areas of her skin.

Her dreads touched them gently.

She had called me *white boy* once and that was the only time she brought it up.

The idea of "race" was weirdly expressed in Detroit, a city where the divide between white and black was so starkly symbolized by one road: 8 Mile. It was as if we each accepted each other's myths, although we never—ever—openly acknowledged them as myths. I'd had to pretend, of course, to be mostly unaware of this which was hard to do, as I'd been schooled in Detroit's past by Charlotte.

I thought of Charlotte, and why she had chosen me.

Patti came over and joined us and I got a good look at the punk buttons on her jean jacket. I was surprised to spot a Yama button there and she must have noticed.

Her hair had been red, but now it was black.

She leaned forward and shook her head and I could see the red beneath the wig.

"Just because I was Yama's bitch for a year doesn't mean I can't sport one of their buttons," she said, as if to the open doorway.

"Don't Look Now, Mr. Roeg, it's Yama's bitch," said Julia. "Roeg, rogue, demon cloud / came upon a red-caped crowd."

Then, as if she had conjured it, a red Camaro (the same bloody shade as her hair) pulled up out front, the doors slammed, and two men walked in. One wore baggy pants and a bright white tank top (wife beater, the Colonel would have called it). The other one—the taller one—wore shorts and a loud orange Hawaiian tee shirt and a heavy gold chain.

They took seats at the bar unceremoniously. The first customers I'd seen in two days. The green propeller lay on the bar in between them. They ordered for each other.

"The brothers are here," said Julia.

"He'll have a Jameson's," the taller one said.

"And he'll have a boilermaker. Jack and Pabst."

The taller one clapped his hands once in front of him and said, *That's right!*

There seemed to be a time-shift around them.

A delayed reaction between their actions—shutting the Camaro's doors, ordering drinks, clapping hands—and the sounds those actions made. A very slight delay, as if they were much farther away than they were and sound had to travel a great distance.

The tall one turned slowly around on his barstool and looked at me slyly, his head bent low and for some reason I thought of the monument to Joe Lewis, known around here as "the Fist," and how the first time I saw it, what moved me wasn't the fist itself, but the part where the arm was severed, which was well above the elbow, cut clean like a terrible amputation, more violent than the fist itself, like a black man's body lynched and hacked apart and hung in the public square for display. That's Detroit. That's how Detroit remembers.

Paul made the drinks and then went back in the storeroom. Rachel had disappeared somewhere, maybe to the bathroom. The shorter man wearing the wife beater came over and stood by our table.

"You seen Rex?" he asked.

"Who's Rex?" Julia said.

"Pooch. Black with a limp and a blind eye. And no tail. Used to come in here when he ran away, which, as he hasn't done for a while, we haven't had to come lookin'. Up and down e-ver-y penny ante street on the northwest side and Rexy nowhere to be found. Laryngitis killed his bark but he's still got spunk. Used to come in here when it was Grandy's, me and Rex, which is probably why he still runs here."

"There was a pack of dogs over at Muirland yesterday. Maybe he's with them," Patti said.

"Shit there's dogs everywhere."

The *Temple of Doom* machine sprung to life and barked out some garbled line from the movie, followed by bells and whistles, and then went silent again.

The shorter guy by the table nodded his head as if in agreement either with the movie line or what the tall one had just said. The sound of a fighter jet, followed closely by another one, screamed across the sky outside and isn't it strange, I thought, how little drones, some not any heavier than a small bird, were more dangerous than those jets.

The shorter one went back over to the bar.

He put his hand on the tall one's shoulder and they walked out.

The green propeller that had been on the bar had, I noticed, disappeared with them.

Tomorrows, why? The Colonel was obsessed with repressing it upon its publication.

I'd read it because he made me. As subversive as it was, he wanted to expose me to the most drastic forms of dissent which he believed took the form of art or literature rather than political speeches or pamphlets or even protests. I suppose he assumed I'd be vaccinated or inoculated against anti-protectorate ideas if I were exposed to them at a young enough age, under his tutelage, so rather than shield me from them he allowed me access to them, to the underground films, the graffiti, the poems, the stories, the captured shortwave radio broadcasts, even the taped confessions of tortured insurgents.

Like I said, I'd gathered more than enough information— just seeing how the propeller exchange worked was more than enough—and so I could and should have left, gone back to my car, driven out of that city, filed my report, and awaited instructions for my next assignment.

And I would have were it not for Rachel, Rachel's hand that I imagined holding. Rachel whose scars had opened my heart to her at first sight, the leader of the sisters it seemed to me, the one who held the keys to the inner world I could sometimes feel or glimpse but never see directly, the one who'd first told me about her kleptomaniac nymphomaniac Karen and who'd asked me a question—*You call this a cigarette?*—that, for some reason, rang in my head for so long, and, finally, Rachel who leaned across the table at hour 41 and asked me if I wanted to go to the Old Miami with her to see Yama.

A mistake.

A glorious mistake.

February 5, 2000

Antony,

Such little rollers they are! They want to crawl so bad you can tell but instead they'll just roll to move from here to there.

Remember I said that I sensed I was being followed? Well I was and probably still am.

The owl kid. But he was either terrible at his job or else they wanted me to know. He turned up everywhere I was and when I confronted him he disappeared and I haven't seen him since, except for feathers.

What do you think that means? Doesn't its weirdness remind you of our time together?

Also: do you remember the antenna? The enormous antenna, on the warehouse?

There were actually more than a ▮▮ or so but you could only see one—the tallest one— from the street. The one with blinking red lights that's said to summon The One Who Comes in the Night. I noticed you noticing it when we went there the second time, during that whole red propeller / green propeller exchange, which was carefully orchestrated for you, of course, down to every last nonsensical, but seemingly cryptic, gesture and action.

Julia almost blew it with her line It's not going to be that easy because the way she rehearsed it was It's not going to be that simple.

You shouldn't have done that. Looked at the flashing red lights.

Did you think we didn't know you'd seen the shrouded person when we had you take those pictures? The look on your face! But by that time it was hard for me to deceive you and I felt a little sorry for you.

The antenna, that's one of the old ones from the protectorate that we repurposed, attaching that circle with the X inside as a symbol, a reminder of what our lives used to be like in the old days, trapped. A person standing with her legs apart and her outstretched arms above her head, forming an X, her feet and hands pushing against the boundaries.

They're scattered all around Detroit once you begin to notice them. But that particular antenna was special because it's more than a symbol, it's a functioning symbol.

I'm only telling you this Antony because from you're in no position to share any information with anyone. How's that for a euphemism? It was actually Jules who came up with the idea to simply re-broadcast as much of the protectorate's archives as remain on a low-watt station. You'd need a transistor radio to pick it up. It's amazing how much crap the protectorate saved, audio files upon audio files of speeches given by the most unimaginative and boring protectorate functionaries. You remember them, right? Growing up they were everywhere.

About those scars on your wrists. You know that we knew—right away—that they were fake, right? We're all-too familiar with scars—me and Julia and Patti—believe me, to be fooled. You must have known about our own scars and figured that, I don't know, we'd be more open or sympathetic if you came in scarred, too. I can't be sure but I'll bet most of what you told us about the Colonel is true.

You were so transparent, Antony.

I think I loved that about you. But it was also dangerous. Dangerous for you.

It was so tempting to believe you, but you were too good to be true. I started right off the bat with that story about Karen the klepto-nympho to see how you'd react but I didn't expect you to listen the way you did and even show interest. God! At the time I thought that you saw through the whole thing and were just toying with me, prodding me to provide more and more details about a person who didn't exist. But as I was telling you about Karen I could see you really were interested, that your interest was genuine. How could you let your feelings show like that and expect to survive? Didn't the Colonel teach you anything?

Rachel

March 7, 2000

Antony,

It terrifies me to think about what you won't be able to remember because of what they're doing to you. Or will you
remember, but differently? I wonder which is worse?

I've interceded as best I can to have them go easy on you,
not like the others, who deserved every bloody thing they got
before the final ███ t. But I never wanted to see you suffer,
Antony, I really didn't. Especially the kind of suffering that
happens where they've got you now.

I'm not cruel. I'm no sadist.

I've been on the other end of things and I have empathy,
I really do, and yet there you were, you came back! You must
have known.

Why did Charlotte pick you?

I know you can't say anything, that's okay. Yama will likely
be involved. They usually are.

The last one was a woman, did you know that? Did they
tell you who'd you'd be replacing when they sent you, or
did they let you think you were the first one? Last year she
walked into Fletcher's just like you. Said she was in Detroit
to document "architecture"!

Oh everyone's so excited about restoring our "ruined"
architecture here! Jules and I knew right away but Paul, well,
Paul had a thing for her.

Short but intense. She seduced him. The first time I've
seen that happen. He had his predilections and weaknesses
but usually his tastes ran in the other direction. In the end
he made the right ███, of course.

It was terrible what Yama did to her body but then again she was a terrible person.

(I had to take tougher measures against the owl kid, to protect myself, but I can't say more about that here.)

We're all tired of the struggle, no matter what side we're on.

I sometimes wonder why the choices, for so long, have been the protectorate, on the one hand, and the insurgency, on the other. Isn't there another way? Other ideas that don't belong to either side? How would Hegel think about it? It's actually something I've wondered a lot about, and so has Julia. We've even talked about leaving, just leaving Detroit and going somewhere else, somewhere remote and just living apart from it all. Utopian, right? But every time we get into it too deep we talk ourselves out of it. The truth is, both of us are too involved already and I doubt Paul and those ▇▇▇ would look too kindly on our defection.

That's the big lie on both sides, isn't it?

That the means—no matter how terrible—justify the ends. As long as those ends are the right ones.

I'm not saying there's no differences.

The protectorate was rotten and fucking psychotic in ways that the insurgents never were. If we've adopted some of their techniques, so to speak, it's only temporary, or so we tell ourselves.

And I'm afraid Antony you've fallen into the hands of those among us willing to use such "techniques" on people like you. Do you remember that other building behind the greenhouse? The black one? I know you're not there because I've been there to look for you but that's where they practiced the protectorate's techniques on people like you, exposing them to ▇▇▇▇▇ and even ▇▇▇▇▇ to derange them enough to reveal things without knowing they were revealing things. It was so abstract except for the blood but even after a while the blood became abstract. And wasn't that why the protectorate succeeded, for awhile, because they'd managed to forge a chain that linked one abstraction to another, each in turn transformed from something concrete and terrible into just an idea?

Do you ever wonder how Detroit became the battleground for much of this? Patti's theory was that it goes back to the '67 riots—Julia called them the 12th Street riots or the insurrection or uprising—which goes to show how right Orwell was about language and power and memory. Julia had a whole history worked out about how the flight of capital from the city created these spaces—*wastelands* she calls them—that were uncontaminated by the politics or ideologies of either side and that people like me and her and Julia naturally gravitated here. Actually, Julia's uncle was in the blind pig on 12th and Rosemount that was raided that night in the summer of '67.

Revolutionary do-it-yourselfers, so to speak. I don't know about that but I do know that I never felt freer than I did in Detroit, and that's one of the things that I loved about it Antony—that I felt free together with you and I can't separate us being in Detroit from us.

For a while I worried that I only loved you because of where we loved each other—this city.

What if it was not each other that we fell in love with, but the circumstances surrounding each other?

Do you realize that either consciously or unconsciously, you wanted us to suspect you weren't who you said you were? When we told you all that Yama nonsense—about the terrible things they'd done to Patti—you didn't seem surprised, and of course it was obvious that you'd heard about them before. I didn't know the full extent of Charlotte's involvement then but I knew that someone had schooled you in Detroit and its secrets and it was so obvious how you tried to pretend you didn't know! But Charlotte didn't tell you everything did she? She didn't warn you about what might happen if you were caught. I wonder if that's why she sent you in the first place, to get caught.

And then the greenhouse, where you were tagged and infected. "You were"—passive voice.

They. We. I.

I led you to the greenhouse.

I think maybe they didn't train you well enough or else they trained you well but you got distracted by xxxxxxxxxx .

I know this letter is long but we were all pretty asexual for a while, and Patti still is. (Do you even want to hear about this?) I knew you wanted to kiss me right away and of course I used that to throw you off, but I didn't think it would be so easy.

I don't know if you saw it or not but by the warehouse there's a small park that's gone to pot but there's a metal sculpture there by Michael Hall, from the early 1970s. It's like a monkey bars but simpler, more melted looking.

Anyway, it's a thing to do it there. To fuck.

Sex on architecture.

Against that sculpture. When we walked by it on the way to the warehouse I thought I felt something—this will sound corny—but I thought I felt something. I felt that I could see myself through your eyes, just briefly. And not just your eyes. I actually became you for a few moments Antony and saw what you saw, and felt what you felt, and what you felt forme, which was very strong. Desire. Lust. That's what it was. I wanted to kiss you again, too, and see where it went from there.

If fucking was a permanent way of life then that's how that sculpture makes you feel. That's what it triggers in you. To just fuck for eternity.

I saw myself walking there beside you and I'll put it squarely: I wanted you to fuck me, against the sculpture. It only lasted a moment, but for that moment I'd become you. That was the strongest feeling; I'm sure there were others but that was the strongest. If I could replay that moment I'd like to see myself again, through your eyes. It was different than seeing yourself in a picture or on video, maybe because it's always through a lens or a screen. But this was through your eyes and they even felt different from mine, the colors of things were slightly different. Not less bright or vibrant so much as a shade darker.

Do you still have the red marble?

Chained to a wall as you most likely are you can't write me back your answer, I know. I wonder: could you speak your answer and have someone write it down? Do you still have a tongue?

It was Jules who told me about the red marbles, told me about their power and then showed me. She bored me to death with her prattle about the Michigan basin and inland saltwater lakes and how the deer, hundreds of thousands of years later, made their way south from Canada by following the salt and sand from those evaporated oceans. I think sometimes she actually believed she was Evie, a lone woman on a dangerous journey and all that. I guess that's the power of *Beyond Blue Tomorrows*—it can make you feel that you are really part of it.

God the boredom of geology!

But the fragility of those marbles and if I'm not making much sense it's because the marbles themselves are incomprehensible and the fact that she willingly gave one to you, through that vent, well that's remarkable I can tell you. Remarkable and terrifying.

Geology is history, right, and yet who cares, really?

You hold a pebble in the palm of your hand and someone tells you it's from before the dinosaurs and even before what they call geologic time, maybe a billion years ago—you are holding in your hand a billion-year old artifact—and it's so banal—a pebble!—and yet also a compressed memory, a piece of a brain.

A little piece of the earth's brain ███ knew you were in the men's room and that this would be our best chance to slip you the red marble undetected, because Paul's people are everywhere. Me and Julia. It was Julia's idea—I wish I'd thought of it—to send you the marble through the vent and of course it all depended on, number one, the vent actually running through and connecting the men's and women's restrooms and, number two, you noticing or caring enough to investigate. We were right about the vent, and we were right about you. I actually saw your fingers as you took the marble. Did he take it, Julia asked, and I tried to sshhh her and we laughed like girls even though it stunk of piss in there, probably because Paul lets guys use the women's restrooms when it's busy on the weekends.

Antony when I got the message that you'd arrived I had no idea. I had no idea what to do or say. To get your attention. My instinct was to be mean with that alligator scale bag. Of all the things! I hadn't received your dossier yet. None of us had.

But we knew about Charlotte.

We knew about The One to Come. Repetition and disorder.

We weren't flying blind. I don't know what told me to curse like I did—that bitch

Karen!—do you remember that? Of course you do. I think I wanted to Does that make sense?

Here's my theory, as of now. Everything's duplicity.

I mean I don't act like I believe it but I do. If I don't trust myself who can I trust?

Not poor old Paul, Chu Chu killer.

None of us knew anything about you other than you'd been sent, like those before you, to learn about how we sabotaged those drones that the protectorate was so obsessed with. We knew of course why you'd chosen Fletcher's. No rocket science there. You're probably wondering why it remained a hub even though your ███ it was a hub. Good question. As long as your side keeps sending people, there will be people like Paul on my side doing the whole drones charade, the whole warehouse charade, not that there's no truth to what we staged for you. There's two sides to everything; that's the terrible truth and I don't know if your side acknowledges it, probably not, but it obsesses my side.

We talk about it all the time. God! Oh well. My hand's getting tired. Detroit's obsession with the protectorate is what's saved us. It works to our advantage honestly. We can as the city changes around us.

Did you feel it? The warehouse, of course. It was real. Don't get to thinking that the whole of everything we showed you, every blind path out on Livernois we sent you, was fake or inauthentic because let me assure you it wasn't, Antony.

It's no longer just you and me Antony. They're finally here and they are beautiful.

There are four of us now. The first one's sleeping right now and the second one is staring at me with her beautiful big eyes, your eyes Antony. But how to keep them safe, to shelter them, not just from people like Charlotte and Paul, but from ideas, from the poisonous ideas of this world?

Can you picture the sun?

Can you picture the drain? Don't dismiss the lowly drain. The sand.

The marble.

If there's a secret way out for you Antony, that's it. Come back Antony!

If not for me then for them? Two girls with your eyes. Creatures like us.

Love, R

Antony

I DON'T REMEMBER WHY OR HOW BUT I KNEW THAT THE annotated manuscript of *Beyond Blue Tomorrows* would be waiting for me at the Old Miami. Maybe Rachel told me. Or Patti. Maybe it had something to do with the red marble and as I'm thinking more carefully about it now I think that's when I knew, as if the marble activated some foreknowledge. And despite the warnings about Yama, that's why I decided to go to the Old Miami. That and the fact that it would allow me to spend more time with Rachel.

By the time Rachel and I had crossed Martin Luther King, Jr. Boulevard, turned left after Orchestra Hall and cut our way through some lots to Cass Ave. I could feel the tug of the place, like some dull magnet pulling gently at my knees and thighs. Rachel took my hand and it was so small. The WELCOME VETERANS lettering on the Old Miami's faded green awning was a reminder that both sides had lost people in previous wars, before there were two sides. There was a light rain so everything was inside tonight rather than out on the scrubby back lawn and a DJ in dressed in all white was on the small stage setting up.

A few people were gathered at the bar. *Let me show you. What they did.*

The bartender wore an Army jacket, her pitch black hair cropped short. The place smelled of gunpowder.

An enormous tattered *Apocalypse Now!* poster with a blood orange sun rising or setting over a jungle carved up by a snaking river filled an entire wall.

There were the usual dirty couches and a stuffed wolverine that had seen better days and several quotes by Diego Rivera and Frida Kahlo chalked in careful cursive on the walls. Framed black and white photographs of fields and spare buildings and horses in an area that I assumed was this place before it was developed. There was a color photo, also, of an accident scene, a red Ford pick-up that had hit a tree square on and a broken arm hanging outside the driver's side window, the hand limp, and it reminded me of one of those Warhol photos—blue photos or red ones—of a car accident, the car upside down on a night road, and there was also an old map of Detroit, in French, and a large metal trap hanging from a chain that was labeled BEAVER TRAP – 1829.

What they did to me.

If I've made too much of Rachel's scars, that's only because they made too much of me. I won't dwell on them except to say that there was something about the light in the Old Miami—a sort of dull green or aqua-marine light—that gave rise to the more intricate patterns and networks in those scars, just beneath the shiny surface. I suppose I had my own scars that were visible too, other than the ones on my wrists, and certainly the bartender did, scars that seemed to glow beneath her green canvas Army jacket.

A group of wiry people were suddenly there at the bar. I hadn't seen them come in.

I'm grateful. They left enough of me.

Four men with stringy black hair down, nearly, to their knees, and a woman with a shocking blonde wig or real hair that suggested a wig.

Were they even real live human beings?

I didn't need anyone to tell me that this was Yama, and that at a place like the Old Miami the band didn't have the privilege of a "green room" to get just drunk enough to play but rather sat at the horizontal bar like everyone else, paying like all the rest of us, trusting the locals not to bother them.

The men were skeletal, their frames so thin and frail that the roar of noise they made later seemed impossibly strong coming from their emaciated bodies.

They stunk of onions.

At some point one of them fell asleep right there at the bar, or appeared to fall asleep.

Do you accept that everything in life will let you down in the end? Rachel whispered in my ear and as strange as that question seemed at the moment—inside the infernal confines of the Old Miami—it made perfect sense, or if not perfect sense then it at least ordered the moment into some sort of recognizable shape. For how old was I when I realized my father was more like an anti-father? That he was against me, not for me? Wasn't it my father who'd convinced me that I was the one who'd *let him down* when, in fact, it was the other way around? How could a man who helped construct and enforce so much order and discipline in the protectorate raise a son who saw nothing but disorder and chaos in everything?

I'm grateful. The thing in the room.

A clatter of plates from the back of the bar suggested food might be on the way, even though no one as far as I knew had ordered anything, but then the bartender, who

I hadn't even noticed had disappeared, re-appeared with a platter full of fried pickles and several small, plastic cups of mustard dip. This seemed to reinvigorate the band, and even the sleeping member lifted his head to partake in a pickle. I wondered then about the supposed danger of Yama, and Patti's stories about how one of them always stayed in the audience as a supposed fan, and as I looked around I wondered who it might be. One of the rich, northern Detroit suburb girls slumming it, already high on Scooby Snacks over in the velvet couched corner? Or in another corner some kids who, in their faded denim grunge hand-me-downs, looked like they were from Downriver, laughing guiltily even though there was no chance in hell their parents would find them here.

"Is this Detroit enough for you?" Rachel asked. "You know, once Yama starts there's no going back."

A small crowd had slowly been gathering. The four skeletal Yama guys at the bar had disappeared and I searched the crowd for the fifth, the planted member, the one who would recruit their next victim, when it dawned on me that this person, this fifth member of the band, was none other than Rachel herself.

It made sense, terrible sense, and I had to be very careful not to let on what I'd surmised. *I remember now. Dear I remember now.*

It was Rachel who'd initiated everything and set the entire wheel in motion, from the moment she approached me at the table at Fletcher's to this end point, right now. Did this mean that she knew who I really was, and why I was really here, infiltrator that I was? I suspected that she did, and everything that happened next depended on how well I could make myself forget that so as not to tip my hand. I remembered how I used to act around the Colonel, before I came around to his vast way of thinking, how I used to pretend to agree with him and all the secret strategies I worked out to disguise my true beliefs and feelings and I supposed some of that kicked in there with Rachel at the Old Miami.

Was her plan to turn me over to Yama so they could exact their torture porn on me? And if so, on whose orders? Paul's? The two guys who'd mysteriously come into Fletcher's, asking about a lost dog? Had those guys come in to ID me, to verify who I really was? What about the guys in the car in front of the church who handed me the Yama flyer in the first place? It all made sense in the absurd way that you can make a series of past events make sense and cohere and so even though I was convinced that Rachel was working with Yama I was anything but confident about what it all meant.

I knew where to look for it. In fact, I didn't have to look at all. I rapped my knuckles on the bar and as the bartender turned to me I noticed that one of her small ears was completely black like a piece of charred wood left over from a fire. Her army jacket had the familiar patches but then a few that I didn't recognize, symbols that I'd never seen before. As absurd as it sounds, I ordered the manuscript as if I was ordering a drink.

"I'll have the *Creatures*," I said.

The bartender winked at me and produced a faded red envelope with the pages inside. I read them right there, standing at the bar, with Rachel next to me lost in conversation with the person next to her. The strange orange glow of the room. The way the soft light seemed to come from everywhere. I'd never really believed the Colonel's hints and insinuations during my childhood that he'd had a hand in creating the book everyone had read, or at least said they'd read. I understood then—reading through the typed pages at the bar—how awful it must have been for the Colonel to have his contributions erased from history, which helped explain why he'd wanted to erase me. Not that his contributions to *Beyond Blue Tomorrows* amounted to much: even if you took it at face value and added up as true all the self-aggrandizing claims he made in the annotations, it still wouldn't nail— let alone tack—his name to the wall of literary history. Of course, the annotations were interesting, to me, on another level, for no matter how much I'd tried to distance myself from the Colonel, or he from me, such mutual rejection is only an idea, an attitude, a way of being in the world. The biological fact remained and despite my generation's gospel of self- cultivation there was no way to un-determine what had been determined: I was my father's son.

I finished the manuscript quickly, slid it into the envelope, and pushed it back across the bar. I didn't need to take it. I didn't need to keep it. Unaffected, strangely. That's how I'd describe what I felt. All those years of rumors and of wondering about the Colonel's contributions to *Tomorrows* but at the end of the day reading it had barely raised my pulse. Rachel turned to me, her face glowing. That moment—it was a moment of pure unadorned happiness and I met her gaze and held it so it wouldn't stop, that blossoming feeling, so it wouldn't go away.

The band was assembling itself on the rickety stage.

Rachel put her hand on my shoulder and whispered in my ear, *it's happening.* Either they were drunk or we all were. The texture of the marble.

That stage: it was really nothing more than a two or three-foot high warped plywood platform just large enough for a drum kit, keyboards, and mic and guitar stands plus amplifiers and speakers. Some bands—just like some writers or movie directors— inhabit their public personas so fully that you sense there's no falsity there at all, no bad faith, and that in fact the public self is no different from the private one which in this case meant that the members of Yama really were *of the devils*, as Patti had said, for why else would their bodies be so emaciated, depleted of life?

They set up their instruments as if walking on the moon or in a vat of invisible molasses, their hair hanging loose and stringy like black threads or beaded into some ropey ponytail, their fingers more knuckley bone than flesh. Of course, they were dressed in the usual black, but such a uniform and *unforgiving* black as if their clothes had soaked up the night. There was a blackness *behind* the blackness.

And there was a sound *behind* the sound. The silence *behind* the silence.

The blackness *behind* the blackness.

I'd heard doom metal before but nothing like this as the band struck and held one dark trembling note, wavering and skipping, sustaining it for minutes as the sound of crickets or something like crickets slowly crept into the empty sonic spaces behind that resolute note, a lonely night of crickets with their little hearts beating in their black bodies. I could feel the dark in a way that really hurt and that pushed outward from my head as if the music was coming from inside me, as if it had been there all along, dormant, waiting to leak out. They held that one note for so long and it got darker and darker and fuller and harsher and I could feel myself sinking into that blackness.

Across the small room I saw the Downriver grunge girls in their retro mini-skirts trying to get signals on their phones but there were no signals in the Old Miami, everyone knew that, knew that it had been constructed out of a kind of metal that, as it turned out, blocked radio signals and satellite signals and signals of other sorts unknown when the building itself was built. The bartender in the Army jacket was making drinks with her eyes closed, it seemed, mixing in too much alcohol and there was a thin haze of smoke collecting just beneath the ceiling. Her fingers reminded me of spider legs.

Above the noise, Rachel asked me what I thought. "Fantastic," I said.

"Fantastic how?" I remember the slight squint of her eyes as she asked.

"The music, the space. It's fantastic."

"That's not a word I'd use to describe it," she said.

"Did you find what you were looking for?" she asked me. I knew what she meant, but how could I possibly answer? Had she known about the manuscript behind the bar? Was that what this had been all about, a maneuver to bring me to the Old Miami to read *Tomorrows* under the spell of Yama?

It seemed as if the drummer had fallen asleep, his head tangled in his ratty hair resting on his snare, his long spindly arms hanging down, his fingers touching the floor. His nails were long and black. If it was true that Rachel was the band's fifth member and that I'd been brought here for a reason (a ruse that began when I was handed the flyers, if not before) then I'd need to leave before Rachel's next move, which I guessed would involve putting something in my drink, although that was just a hunch, for I had no real idea of how she'd go about turning me over to Yama. If nothing else, I'd learned that the Detroit insurgents were more confident and established than I'd imagined and that Rachel, at least, had known from the beginning why I was really here. Suddenly I couldn't breathe. I tried to touch the room with my fingers but it made no sense. The frame of a door. The drummer's fingers touching the floor. The bartender doubled and then tripled moving at different speeds against the black noise pouring out from the band. It's hard for me to write about this now. I'm getting closer to the black hole of what happened.

"I've got to go," I said to Rachel.

"What. Why? They haven't even started yet. Not properly."

"I can't stay and I think you know why," I said.

It was a dangerous thing to say, yet I felt I owed her that much, at least, a little bit of honesty at the end of this cat-and-mouse game that we'd been playing. She smiled and nodded. Her scars looked more beautiful than ever and I regretted that I wouldn't be able to touch them.

"I understand," she said. "Would you like to go somewhere else?"

"You know I can't," I told her, although her request surprised me.

She'd allowed me to see how the drone sabotage happened, allowed me in on the whole absurd and absurdly complicated propeller exchanges and it was then, during the last moments at the Old Miami with Yama starting up their devil music and Rachel sitting beside me that I realized that the *Temple of Doom* pinball machine was just a ruse, a way to disguise instructions so they sounded like lines from the movie, right there in broad daylight, for anyone to hear, and when I went back later and reconstructed my time at Fletcher's I could understand why Paul spent so much time tinkering with the machine because a lot of what happened in that bar coincided with supposedly random lines of movie dialog. When I got up to leave I noticed a slight quiver, a gentle disruption, in Yama's "song" which was still that ridiculously long single note and I wondered if they'd already known, before Rachel brought me before them, that I was the one, that I was to have been the one.

I'm so grateful.

They left enough of me.

The insurgents. I remember how, at one point in my life, I wanted to be everything the Colonel was not, and this had nothing to do with politics or loyalty to the protectorate but rather his confidence, the sense or feeling that what he was doing was natural and correct and necessary and that doubt was not only a sign of weakness but of something worse, of immorality. I suppose that's why I'd befriended Thomas, the doubter, who looked for proof (or so I thought at the time) of the protectorate's inflated claims about its success and, upon finding none, embarked on a journey of skepticism and doubt. The point is, I'd become everything I'd hated about the Colonel and I'd arrived at a kind of moment when this became clear to me, so radically clear.

Does she carry a banner?

That one note forever.

My sister.

Once again that soft green pasture in Kentucky visiting my cousins with the horses and their thick steak-like tongues opened up in my mind, the way one of those horses would always come over to me at the fence, the way its impossibly shaped head and cue ball eyes would meet me—I must have been six or seven—and how even then I knew instinctively, or at least had a sliver of knowledge, that nature had no ideology, although at the time I probably just felt safe there, that there was nothing in the horse's grass-filled stomach, or the blank pasture or the trees or the brook or the cedar split-rail fence or the skies that could hurt me, at least not in the way the Colonel could hurt me.

But it was more than that because the natural world had no ideas, no ideas that curl themselves into a terrible logic that would lead to anger and hate and violence.

The moss, the trees, the pasture, the clouds, the insects: they were idea-less and I found such peace and comfort there and I remember taking off my shoes and standing barefoot at the edge of the pasture so I could feel the grass and the sandy, damp earth on the bottoms of my feet.

If the Colonel had his way, I was sure all this would be paved over with meaning and intention, not just the intention to survive and propagate—which is nature's goal—but to exist with a force of will, a will shaped and guided by ideas, ideas that, in turn, fueled the will that gave rise to them.

It was only later, when I was a young man, that I understood why it was the Colonel had been so obsessed with Marx, even though he and the protectorate were fighting to extinguish every citizen who harbored Marxist beliefs. It was the specific arguments of Marx that fascinated him, the impersonal and inevitable force of history he found expressed there, as if Marx had everything right except that he chose the wrong winners and losers in history. The horse's warm snot in the palm of my hand from which his rubbery, hairy lips had snatched acorns knew nothing of any of that, and if I romanticized the natural world and its mysteries and rhythms during those summers visiting Kentucky, that's only because I didn't yet understand how easily it all could be taken away.

Yama's single note song still rang in my ears, more like a signal than a song and a darkness flooded in and obscured everything. It was the most beautiful, dangerous feeling in the world. I thought about Rachel and how she'd explain what became of me to the others and I wondered what sort of danger they'd be put in by the report I was going to write about what happened in and around Fletcher's.

I don't remember what happened that night, after I left the show.

The next day I was back at Fletcher's. It was as if time had skipped ahead, as if the hours of the night simply did not exist. Rachel was there, at a table, wearing a red beret.

"You missed quite a show," she said. "Where'd you run off to?"

"Yama scared me away," I joked, but of course it was true. I sat down across from her.

"You left this behind," she said, sliding a red propeller over to me.

"After you split Yama played another song, which was also just one note. And then a third. The whole concert was three songs, and it lasted three hours. The skanks fromDownriver left early, of course. I stayed until the end and was there for last call. I walked home alone afterwards, it was around 3 in the morning, which took me by the old train station. There were people with flashlights exploring it. I thought back to what Julia told us about her uncle in Albania in the 1970s and the destruction, and how you'd said something like that couldn't happen in this country, but of course it did, and that bothered me, it bothered me when you said it and then even more later and I haven't been able to stop thinking about it, really. I've been wondering about it and now you're back so we can settle it maybe."

"Settle it how?"

I don't want to talk about how I was abducted, and what happened after that. I'm told that the only way to heal is through the story of how this happened. But I don't believe in healing, not any more.

A crack in the wall. The frame of a door.

On my way back to the old church. I'd been warned of course, but then I'd been warned of so many things that turned out to be harmless: the wild dogs, The One Who Comes in the Night, Paul even. I wanted to see the church again. Its ruined insides and yet still a place of order. What they did to me. Something dragging itself across sand leaving a trail.

That one note we could play for you forever. The rest of your life extending like one long night. They said that to me as if it was a granite-hard fact that everyone in the world had learned to recognize except for me.

I slid the red propeller back to Rachel. She touched it with her fingers without taking her eyes off me. And then suddenly there was Paul. Had he been in there the whole time, listening, and me not noticing? He was behind the bar drying his enormous hands with a white towel. He barely looked at me. Could I write a report that would spell the end of Rachel? It was the Colonel who'd taught me that sentimentality was the biggest obstacle to political will, by which he meant the political will of those who identified with the protectorate.

Maybe it was his fear of sentimentality, of too much *feeling*, that led him to switch between the warm father cooking up a slow breakfast on some mornings to the cold, sarcastic lecturer who made me feel like the poorest excuse for a son in the universe. In fact, nostalgia had never been part of the protectorate's ideology, and in this way they learned from and broke with their fascist predecessors, for whom nostalgia, tradition, and the old ritual customs had been so fundamental.

Instead, the theorists of the protectorate were future oriented, appealing not to the primitive desire to restore order, but rather to the desire to create a *new* order. And in a weird way it had worked all too well on me because now my memories of the Colonel's tender side were anything but golden as I couldn't help but recall those moments without also recalling their opposite: his furious face, his marble-like knuckles as he clenched his fists, the shape of his body settling down in the kitchen-table chair for one of his hours-long lectures. There was no disentangling them. The past for me was so poisoned I dare not linger there long.

I'm so grateful. I could stand.

Does she carry a banner?

Even though I was prepared for it and didn't want to believe it—not after having met her—I was pretty sure Rachel's long, personal discourse was part of a ruse. Our long, sometimes flirtatious conversations had likely allowed glimpses of who'd sent me to Detroit and why, and yet, of course, I'd also gleaned a lot from our conversations, information that Charlotte expected to read about in the report I was supposed to write. That was one of the absurd protocols of the protectorate: put it in writing so that the reader wouldn't be susceptible to the very sorts of affect mining we'd used to collect the information from the insurgents in the first place.

Put another way: people like Charlotte were afraid that people like me would detect their *true feelings* about whatever report we were delivering. And it worked the other way, too, because theoretically the written word concealed emotional intent: my Detroit report could be read free of the background affect noise generated by delivering it face to face.

"I'm going back to that church," I said to Rachel. Paul stopped what he was doing and looked over at me, as if he just noticed I was there.

He wasn't so gigantic after all, I thought.

I could stand.

I could walk.

That one note forever.

I think we all three realized that the game was up and I wondered if we could just talk to each other on level ground, so to speak.

"You've been warned," said Paul, coming over to the table. He looked me in the eyes, maybe for the first time. I suddenly knew that if I left—if I simply walked out of Fletcher's—I'd probably never come back.

"Come on, Paul. We both know," Rachel said. Her red beret had taken on the bright clarity of a Cardinal.

He looked at Rachel as if searching for approval, and she nodded.

"You'll be followed," he said, "or someone will already be there waiting for you." Of course, I had no way of knowing—not then—whether or not he was bluffing.

Maybe I never would. As I stepped out the door back onto Livernois I heard the weird, digitized voice of Indiana Jones, as if he too was warning me.

The Colonel's Letter

Son,

Anthony, although you've chosen against that name: Antony. Tonight, I am going to hang myself from the Swan Creek Bridge.

I've kept tabulations on what you've become, and what you've done, and where you are.

At least where you are now you won't be able to squirm out of listening to me.

Do I find it ironic (wasn't that a favorite word of yours, or was it just your detached disposition to the world that made it seem so?) that this letter finds you in the hands of the torturers you euphemistically called the insurgents? By calling them that—by adopting the name they called themselves—you legitimized their "cause" of course. From what I've heard, they really know how to use pliers and needles in creative ways, as you no doubt are discovering. Flesh of my flesh. It's too bad Michelle isn't here to weep for you.

I'm told they've spared your eyes, the better to read this with.

"The Colonel"—as you always have insisted on calling me even though I have asked you to call me Father or even Dad—is only one of my titles.

I can tell you this now, and also this:

Your sister. Two years older than you. You didn't know. The question I'd like you to think about is, did she? If, in your short time in Detroit, if you loved Rachel in a way that exceeded the natural boundaries of brotherly affection, you are certainly not to blame, are you?

Fucking your sister is only fucking your sister if you know she's your sister.

So, let's say you didn't. But what about her? I can't help but entertain the idea that she'd been told who you were before you arrived at Fletcher's.

Charlotte sent you there at my request, although no doubt she had her own special reasons. Were I not going to use this rope on my lap I'd tell you about Charlotte's many masks, her fascination with nomenclatures during the protectorate's formative, theoretical years, the bounty of her disguises and ruses, the pleasure it gave her to slip into Detroit in disguise to create her own mythology. Like the rest of us she'd been under the spell of Lacan and his nonsensical theory about the uncanny where, he says, we lose the ability to distinguish pleasure from displeasure. The most amazing thing was how she created rumors of her own self, the creature that comes in the night or what have you, creating her own mythology within the insurgency by showing up at the right places and whispering the right things. You can tell a story a hundred different ways and it's still the same story, or is it the other way around?

I used to have a voice too, Antony. I was a writer, just not of the sorts of books you value so highly. Is it ego, at last, that prompts me to write you? To bend your thoughts back to a document that I had no small part in producing? If *A Report on Beyond Blue Tomorrows* turns out to be a disappointment, well, so have you. To wit: you never really cared about your mother, did you? Did you ever ask me once to talk about her, or am I forgetting something?

Had you ever bothered to ask me about my early days in what you call the protectorate, then you'd know that it wasn't easy. None of it was easy. None of it came naturally. Not that any of us believed in anything like human nature in the first place. I was the one who read Lenin most closely and carefully. "The working class must break up, smash the ready-made state machinery, and not confine itself merely to laying hold of it," he wrote. It was my idea to detour this insight—which despite its power still reeked of romanticism and sentimentality—into something we could all get behind. Take out the working class part and replace it with us. *Us* Antony. Us the smashers-up, the destroyers.

Leave nothing to rebuild. Clear a space—a real, physical space that would give rise to a psychological one—for our ideas to take root and grow. This was all before you were born of course. Before I met Michelle.

You were born, fucker.

You were born and it wasn't easy and you never once asked about Michelle.

But then how could you ask about a person whose name you don't even know or care to know? Your generation always was so very introspective: "self-care" did you call it? You elevated narcissism to the level of virtue. Even the insurgency itself was introspective, defensive. At least we in the protectorate had a vision for change and cared about the shape of the world beyond ourselves, for isn't imposing your will on someone better than having no will to impose?

The force, son, of an idea shaped into violence is preferable to no idea at all. How would you know that she pronounced her name Mee-shell, or that she lost her hair at age 20, or that she wrote poetry, or that a dog bit off half her pinky when she was a girl? You think, perhaps, that I was a poor father because I was only playing a role that had been forced on me and that my real devotion was to the protectorate and that my love for that— for that *idea*—left no room for *you*, or any other human being. And yet what if I told you, Antony, that I waited for you. I waited for you to become a son in the way sons should, to show some affection, to take my hand on those river walks, to laugh spontaneously at something I said, to come into my bed at night when you were frightened, to ask for help with something, to say you loved me.

Do you remember the basement, I wonder? The typewriters I showed you, as a child, in hopes that in recognizing the mediums I used to create our manifestos you might take an interest yourself. How many opportunities like that you let slip away. Rather than ask about the machines, or my writing process, or why I used typewriters in the first place you simply yawned, as I recall. Yawned, Antony! There you were, in the theorist's lair, and as I watched your glassy, rodent-like eyes it was clear how little interest you took. Your lids drooped as I explained the details and intricacies of those machines: the delicate weight and balance of the strike bars, the counterfeited serial numbers to prevent tracing, the elegance of the carriage return bars and their spring action perfection.

I even offered you the rare privilege of touching the keys on one of the machines, the one I'd use to compose the "First and Last Orders" manifesto which had such a profound effect on those who carried out the Fisher incident, and how did you react? By placing your trembling hand just above the keys, as if actually touching them might infect you somehow, Antony. As if they were *dirty* things imprinted with bad ideas when in fact it was *your ideas* that were corrupt and that, as I soon came to see, would lead you into the trap Charlotte had set for you.

If I told you, Antony, that I have spared so many, many more lives than I had any right to, would that make any difference in whatever moral calculation you use to judge those whose views are different from your own? I have grown into a monstrous legend in your own mind. Do you think I'm not aware that you still refer to me as "The Colonel" and who do you think that is fooling anyway? Do the people you spend your time with believe in caricatures, because that's precisely what you have made of me.

But I am not some hideous creature. I'm no monster.

You claim to have come around to our way of thinking and yet you spend your time gathering useless information about these minor pockets of resistance. If you bothered to give one moment's thought to *my* life, *my* sufferings then perhaps it would have helped you to understand your own better.

The suffering of others, son. Do you think you are the only one with doubts?

Could you ever for a moment look out beyond the glare of your own self to see others—to really see them? Or do you think reading books about other lives is enough? Our generation talks of empathy—which I'll admit you have fetishized in a way that even I myself find alluring. No doubt you developed attachments to the idea of others, but what about real people? You saw me as an abstraction: the idea of a father, or should I say the idea of a failed father. I fit that archetype quite nicely, and every word I said, every gesture, I suspect, only further confirmed your ideas about me and buried me deeper in your mind as a monster.

You've lathered me in thick hot black tar and at some point that's all I became to you. TarMan. TarColonel. TarFather. Even thinking of me got your thoughts stuck in the tarpit of me, am I right? And so then you stopped thinking of me. Son, I could feel my disappearance from your brain.

If you succeed in finding my annotations on *Beyond Blue Tomorrows* then maybe you'll see the hand I played— Michelle and I played—in shaping history. If Michelle were still alive she would confirm the enormity of my contributions in crafting the final form and meaning of *Tomorrows*. I never wanted to be an author, son, not in the way you did, and yet which one of us has produced a document as subtle and lasting as *Tomorrows*? Granted I was not the author *per se* of the book, and yet without my involvement I hardly think the book would be worthy of multiple readings, each one revealing a new dimension, a new set of meanings, a new discursive field (as you might say, using your own in-flated way of speaking.) Michelle never revealed the name of the author to me. For a time, I suspected she herself wrote *Tomorrows*. And yet it's my notes and annotations that you'll find in that archive in Detroit. Why?

Why, because Michelle entrusted me with the telling of the story surrounding the book and although it's not for me to suggest her reasons, do you have it within you, son, to find the generosity in your imagination to fathom the possibility that your mother recognized *in me* a talent for bringing forth the all the potential readings that lay fallow in the book? I (practically from the end of a rope) can picture you now condemning me to yet another circle of hell for subsuming Michelle's voice into my own. For why are the annotations mine and not hers? Where is her voice, the voice of your mother? If I told you that I withheld her voice for the simple reason of not wanting to give you the pleasure of Michelle as Michelle—and not as I rendered her—would you think that even too perverse for me, or would it only confirm your bad-faith judgment of who and what I am?

Was I happy that your mother decided to publish *Tomorrows* as an anonymous "text" (as you would call it) without acknowledging our role in editing and even rewriting parts to make it lean, lasting, and for the ages? Of course not. And yet I understood all too well her reasons. I've made sure the annotated version survived and if your sister is anything like your mother—which I'm counting on—then I'm betting it will eventually see the light of day. Why? Because it reflects on her in some way and stakes her, however tenuously, to history. It's simply too tempting: how could Rachel not make public a legendary book whose origins can be traced back to her father? To your father. What, are you growing weary even now? Are your *basement eyelids* drooping? Does the machinery of my thoughts bore you as did the machines upon which they were composed? A hundred upon a hundred manifesto pamphlets I wrote and *now* all you care about are my annotations on another person's book!

And to think how patient I was with you! Of course, you've likely forgotten our time together working the backyard garden. You must have been 12 or 13. In an effort to cultivate some sort of bond with you I had you read aloud passages from *Beyond Blue Tomorrows*, very specific passages, hoping that you might detect my voice in them. Your own father, on his knees before you working the black earth (even wearing that ridiculous denim "gardening shirt" you'd given me as a Christmas gift) listening for any sign in your voice, any twinge of recognition that the words you were reading were penned not by the book's anonymous author, who you along with all the soft minds of your generation worshipped, but *by me*, the Colonel, as you say. Fuck the annotations—my voice was there in the book itself, the primary text as they say. And yet you stood there, son Antony, casting your cold shadow over me in the garden, reading to me the very words I had smuggled into *Beyond Blue Tomorrows*, words that had moved so many readers, and I received not a moment's recognition from you there in the garden, not a *shadow's flicker* of recognition.

You've characterized me to others as distant, aloof, cold. Insofar as that's the case then this was merely a reflection of your own attitude towards me.

I did love your mother.

As for Rachel, she needn't detain us. There are certain facts you can't reveal, not even in a suicide note. Besides, if Rachel hasn't earned the right to know who her mother was, then you certainly haven't either. Rachel was born before I met Michelle and was, as was customary back then when the mother was not of the protectorate, abandoned to the arm of the protectorate that took care of such things.

I never wanted your sister. Not like I wanted you, son.

I loved you because I loved Michelle.

I didn't love Rachel because I didn't love the woman who bore her.

I couldn't help myself. I was true to one fixed idea that was Michelle. You, with your disabled loyalties and scattered principles, can't possibly understand that, can you?

Dad/ The Colonel / Raúl

Rachel's Note

ANTONY LEFT THE OLD MIAMI AFTER HAVING READ *Beyond Blue Tomorrows* only to be abducted a short time later. I left the Old Miami with the manuscript in an envelope marked "Number 12" and went back to Fletcher's where I packaged it up in one of the drone boxes that Julia then delivered to me, much later. I thought hard about how to format the Colonel's annotations, which were written in neat blue ink in the margins and on the back of the manuscript pages.

I thought about footnotes, and then endnotes.

I thought about trying to recreate the Colonel's marginal comments in the margins themselves. I thought about facsimiles and copies. I thought about palimpsests. About psychologies of reading. About phenomenology. Against complexity, simplicity won out. I re-typed the manuscript, changing nothing, except: the Colonel's annotations are rendered in their own font beginning with the line, That's how the document.

Beyond Blue Tomorrows

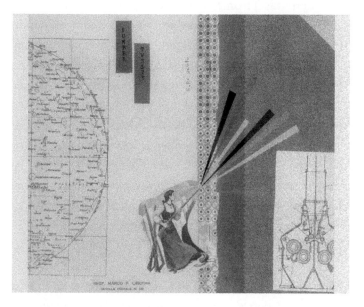

In her mind's eye Evie has an image of the well:
an enormous red brick circle in the middle of the
desert, ranging in height from knee-high to as
tall as a tree. Drifting dunes have shaped its
exposures, the windward portion where the sand
duned up the wall is shallower while on the leeward
side, the sand gullied out, much taller. Even as
Evie pictures it, it continually shifts between
shades of red in the bright desert light, as if in
response to some unknown stimulus.

That's how the document, which came to me second-hand, begins. Calling it a "document" was the first problem, and everything bad flowed from that. We should have called *Beyond Blue Tomorrows* what it was: fiction. Which is to say that at the beginning I questioned its origins, if not its authenticity. Evie's story *felt* true—even as fiction. But where was it from? Who was the author? What was the text's ideology? Whose side was it on? We had been conditioned by our era to see it through the lens of irony, of happy paranoia. We suspected everything. Nothing was exempt. We assumed the story was winking at us; of course it was. How could it not, how could it possibly be serious? No one wrote stories like this anymore— stories with horses and deserts and mysterious travellers. It wasn't that the story it told seemed beyond the realm even of fiction but rather its genre was confused—a western? a spy novel? a metaphysical slow burn? Besides, all those genres had been discredited. Who, these days, could lose themselves in such stories?

```
Evie thinks about this now as she rides Red deeper
into the desert. It's midday, the sun above her
hidden behind a thin layer of vapor, the same layer
of vapor that was always there. The smell of tall,
dry grass, and of the horse. The plump, black flies
that gather around its wet snout. The gentle sound
of metal on metal in her satchel comforts her. She
reflects on the first part of the details of her
mission:

    • approach the well across the desert from the
      east
```

- avoid the wooden bridge that leads across the riverbed

- avoid the flat, shallow rocks that look like burned faces

- when close, observe the well for a day before moving in on it

- traverse the circumference of the well until the discolored stone is located

- at this point, climb the well wall and secure the beacon

This is the first part of the two-part directive. Evie understands that the well varies in size and depth, depending on what sources you consult. Because there are no direct visual reproductions of the well, she has to rely on two types of sources: what the agency has told her, and what she has found on her own, in the old survey books she located in deep storage.

And even these are unreliable and at variance with each other, as some depictions show the well as very tall and imposing while others depict it as being low to the ground, overgrown with grass and shrubs to the extent that it looked more like a circular mound than a stone well.

And, of course, the dating is all over the place. The well is either very old, or relatively new—just made to look old— depending on which sources you consult. Evie remembers two lines she read in one of her books, one of the books she had smuggled out of the archive. It went something like *Knowledge, defined conventionally, always proceeds in the same direction, from the subject to the object. But today a process of reversion emerges—today the object wakes up and reacts, determined to keep its secret alive.* What does this mean? Evie wonders, even as she has a very strong sense of what it does mean. As she lowers herself off Red so that he can graze and so that she can water him, she turns the phrase over again and again in her mind, determined to keep its secret alive. Does the well have determination? she wonders. Does it have secrets? She knows that it does, for that is why she has been sent out here in the first place, to "repair" it, a term she has always assumed was a euphemism for "to fix its leaky secrets." The well had been damaged. Its contents leaking. But what were those contents? Not water. Not fuel. Something else entirely.

There could be endless variations of the story. That's one of the things that attracted and terrified Michelle. A mutation, she called it once. She liked the way it changed on the page, like the sand or the desert itself. And I also came to see Evie's story as something that, if left uncorrected, could leak out and change shape and meaning beyond our control. Transforming in ways that we couldn't anticipate. *The way children do*, Michelle said out of the blue one day, as if we'd been secretly thinking the same thought.

When she reaches the trees, enormous Savannah Oaks in tall yellow grass surrounding a stagnant pool of brown water, she dismounts, waters the horse from the pannier, shakes out her blue scarf that she has used as a headband and scans the horizon behind her with binoculars for signs of him. She has detoured so far from her initial instructions that there is no hope for redemption, even if she believed in such a thing, as if one needed to be redeemed for simply trying to survive. In the distance she sees a line of rising dust from the desert floor and understands that he is, at most, three hours behind her. He can likely see the stand of trees, if not her, and of course knows that this is where she has stopped. The horse has been grazing on the leafy tops of the grass and Evie tends to its front ankle, damaged by the hidden barbed wire from near the beginning of their journey.

The bandage, crusted black in dried blood, comes off like parchment paper. Evie gently dabs the torn skin beneath with water and wraps the ankle in a new strip of fabric while the horse tries to eat her hair. The wound is worse than she thought and Evie imagines—for the hundredth time—the possibilities of what will happen when the horse is no longer able to continue.

```
She has murdered many things before, but never a
horse.
```

Neither Michelle nor I liked the idea of Evie as a killer. How can you identify with a character like that? It was my idea—against Michelle's wishes—to cut the pages immediately following the "She has murdered many things" line. Michelle's suggestion that if Evie had been a man I wouldn't have felt the need to excise her violence was absurd, of course. Like everyone else in those days I'd evolved beyond such binaries. Michelle's charges that I felt "protective" of Evie were likewise curious. In the end my views prevailed and *Tomorrows* was published without the specifics of Evie's murders.

```
In the distance there appears a black outcropping
of soft-looking, rounded rocks, about an hour's
ride away, and it is from there that she will stage
her ambush on the man following her, not killing
him but wounding him, disabling him so that she
can take him with her to finish what she started.
She is halfway to the black rock outcropping and in
the rhythm of the horse's gait her mind swells sea-
tide-like up into the future and then retreats back
into the past. She imagines that the man pursuing
her is in the past for no other reason than that he
is behind her, and that the rocks in the distance
are in the future because they are in front of her.
She takes a carrot from her satchel and feeds it
to the horse as it walks and presses the palm of
her hand on its head and she the vibration of the
crunch. Across her shoulder is her rifle and hidden
```

in the heels of her boots are the two vials with the tightly coiled codes inside.

She is far enough ahead of him now that she can slow down, bringing her blue roan Nakota to a slow walk.

The rocks aren't black after all, but sand colored. They, like the wall, shift colors.

Evie dismounts, unsaddles the horse (she thinks of the horse's name as Red in her head, although it has no name), waters it, feeds it more carrots and several palmfuls of dry corn, scrambles to the highest outcropping, and scans the horizon for him.

He is there, midway between the horizon and where she is, something more than a black speck on a black horse, but not much.

He is too far away to wound, and too close to run from.

Michelle was the first to read the manuscript. It was, after all, her job to detect and scoop up texts like this that circulated unauthorized samizdat-like. During that time there was little care or interest in who the author was, the protectorate itself was so intent on expunging even the faintest traces of personality that interest in authorship would have been seen as a betrayal. The text was one of many so-called "desert stories" circulating then, stories that shared similar elements (tropes, Michelle called them) involving animals (usually horses), deserts (of course), female protagonists, and, for some reason, obscure structures such as wells (as in *Tomorrow*'s case), greenhouses, wooden towers, tunnel systems, and reservoirs.

She acquired it and immediately suppressed it until it became clear that there was no other choice than to publish it. My pre-protectorate background was in finance: the hiding ("sheltering") of vast amounts of capital for clients whom I never met, in locations I had never visited.

I was head-hunted, as they say, by Michelle's associates, who doubled my commission and put me up for one year (to be extended upon successful editing of what came to be known as the *Evie Report*, and finally just *EVIE*, and then briefly *DuneTime* before, finally, reverting back to its original title: *Beyond Blue Tomorrows*) in a basement apartment near Amis Square. As I am a man of few relations, it was easy for me to move from Detroit to New York and to find my life there in the continual buzz that is that city as natural for me as life anywhere else I had lived.

The document presented its problems, not least of which it did not have a through line, *per se*. This isn't exactly true, but true enough. This hadn't been an issue for Michelle and wasn't what made her fear the manuscript. No, it wasn't the lack of narrative coherence that menaced Michelle (in fact, too much narrative tidiness would suggest that the report, like so many others, was a fraud, an imitation of a real report) but rather something else, and here is where things get tricky. Michelle understood, as I would come to as well, that Evie's story was radically dialogic, something she had become attuned to while taking a class with Julia Kristeva, who had introduced her to Bahktin's notion of dialogic versus monologic texts, texts which were closed off to interpretation and commanded One True Meaning. *Beyond Blue Tomorrows*,

Michelle saw, was subversively open and unencumbered by the myth of the author: it was anonymous. Lacking an author-function, it lacked a ready-made interpretive compass. And its meanings were open or, as Michelle put it to me: everybody knows that the Big Bad Wolf is universally bad, but is Little Red Riding Hood completely innocent?

Tomorrows, Michelle told me, was like the girl in the fairy tale: a question mark. There were other ambiguities, too: the lack of chapter headings, the sudden shifts in time, the genre switches that didn't seem intentional, the pacing, and of course the implied, subversive politics.

But none of these stood out to me as fundamental to the report's failure as an intelligence document in Michelle's eyes. One night over drinks that had emboldened me—this would have been about four months into my residency, as I had come to think of it, at the agency—I asked her straight out why she had shelved the report. Her answer was simple and direct, although it nearly put an end to our evening. *I didn't shelve it*, she said, *I saved it*. She said this with an alarm in her voice that I've not heard since, and while to say that my question to her almost put an end to our drinking together would be a lie, it is the case that we never drank again *like that*.

Although Michelle never told me what to change about the report, she was very clear about what process, what procedures, to use. From observing her in action at the agency, dealing with other field reports, white papers, and historical narratives, I came to understand quickly that this was how she operated, from a procedural point of view.

I understood this and admired it, intuitively, because in the virtual world of commerce and futures and exchange that I had come from, we also operated procedurally, as it were.

In Michelle's case—which meant in the agency's case—this meant attacking the manuscript not from the outside, but from within. I was not to change individual words, for instance, but rather to examine their habitat on the page, and work from there outwards in an effort to detect any residual feeling left over by the author. It was affect mining before we called it that.

She is far enough ahead of him now that she can slow down, bringing her blue roan Nakota to a slow walk. Evie lays in wait for the person who's been tracking her. The outcropping of rocks fades into the distance behind her. The landscape of the savannah is such that she can't see the person behind her anymore, so she rides until she finds a small stand of clustered trees and stops there. She feeds and waters Red and pulls off her cracked leather boots, checks the metal heels for the coiled files and then uses the same brush she uses on Red to take the dust off her boots. She undresses, shakes the sand from her clothes, puts them back on, and relaxes beneath a tree.

She figures she has three hours, at least.

Red nuzzles her collar then backs off and sleeps.

Evie slowly, out of habit unshackled from the burden of intention or thought, oils her Winchester SRC rifle, blowing out the dust from around the breechbolt. She unscrews the buttplate where the pewter vial of poison is hidden and shakes it

just to hear it. She reassembles the gun and
rests her head back against the tree. There was
a time when Evie would have hunted someone like
herself, a saboteur. She had turned against the
agency not out of disillusionment but rather out
of curiosity.

Here, too, is an example of how I could—if I had pressed
it—justify myself as author of *Tomorrows*. Or should I say,
the *absence* of an example. For it was my idea to cut a fair
amount of pages clarifying Evie's relationship to "the agency."
Michelle—concretist that she was—felt it was important for
the reader to understand the whats and wherefores of it all
against my theory that all great art is, at its heart, ambiguous at best. Again here Michelle invoked the surprisingly
familiar charge that men could "afford" to be abstract as a
result of the accumulated leisure from generations of prerogative and privilege, as if women couldn't be abstract, too.
Michelle countered, as I recall, that I was simply dressing
up my personal preference as ideology.

Evie's entire life—everybody's—had been lived under
the spell of that far structure, immense and ever
widening in her imagination. She had been chosen as
the one to venture out to repair it not because of
her distinctiveness, she knew, but rather because
she is the very last person you would imagine
making this journey.

She awakens with a start.

She can feel the man's presence close by.

With trained patience and deliberation she rises,
her back against the tree.

X

From her perch upon the rocks in the hot sun, Evie
sees for the first time the man following her is not
alone. Behind him, so far away it appears from her
vantage to be nothing more than a speck of dust,
is someone or something else. And for the first time
Evie contemplates this: that the man trailing her
is unaware, perhaps, that he too is being trailed.

If she has been sent out here to the frontier to
repair the well, and the man following her has
been sent to follow her, then does that mean that
the person following the man—or following them
both—has also been sent? Evie understands that the
syndicate that has assigned her this repair mission
has reason to have her followed and monitored, but
do they also have reason to have the one who has
been sent to follow her followed, as well? Or has
someone else sent him, the second man? (In Evie's
mind she thinks of the man tracking her as the first
man, and the man—if it is a man—following him as
the second man.) Evie is on an area of flat rock
atop the perch and above her several vultures move
in a slow, unsteady circle, black wings against a
blue sky.

She thinks of her father, who taught her first how
to break a horse, those days when the horse was

there in front of your eyes all day, talking to it as it learns to respond to your voice. And yet her memories are not with the horses, really, but with her father, whose job it was to transport the horses, once broken enough to be "finished" and given over to their owners.

These long, often multi-state rides down into the southern territories are what Evie remembers, her father's tattered blue flannel shirt sleeve flapping in the wind as he rested his arm on the open window frame as he drove with his other, his tanned, marble-knuckled hand not so much gripping the wheel as guiding it, the static-y radio stations coming in and going out as they made their way through the foothills of the northern region and then across the great rivers and then into steeper foothills yet and eventually across the mountains and into the southern plains.

It was near the end of my first full week of verifying the manuscript that I detected, or thought I detected, the gendered voice of the author in *Tomorrows*. I had, in business school, fallen under the spell of Adam Smith's *Theory of Moral Sentiments* (1759) and specifically his concept of the invisible hand of the market. "The rich," he wrote, "are led by an invisible hand to make nearly the same distribution of the necessaries of life, which would have been made, had the earth been divided into equal portions among all its inhabitants, and thus without intending it, without knowing it, advance the interest of the society." What interested me wasn't so much whether or not such an invisible hand actually existed, but how one might go about detecting it, and so I was always on the lookout for it, in actuarial tables, in stock indices, in employment data, in market structure patterns, in mergers and acquisitions, and, specifically, in price elasticity of demand. In the 1890s, economist Alfred Marshall had suggested that "the only universal law as to a person's desire is that it diminishes but this diminution may be slow or rapid," and those were the words I returned to when sniffing out the scent of the invisible hand of *Tomorrows'* author.

It was in tag questions that I first detected the voice of the author, hidden beneath the false voice of the implied author, questions such as, *she was being followed, wasn't she?* and *she couldn't pull the trigger, could she?* In these declarative statements, turned into questions via the tagged phrases at the end (*wasn't she?*) I actually heard the voice of the author, across the pages of the desert of Evie's journey. For at the heart of the problem of *Beyond Blue Tomorrows* is Evie's journey on horse and then on foot, to repair the well, an undefined structure that persists—like a gap that's never closed—always retreating on the horizon of the report. I had become interested in the report because it felt so fresh— even subversive. The problem became, for me, that the well exerted a weird gravity on my mind in that the closer Evie came to it the faster my thoughts came, too, as if the well was not only tugging at her (and the man following her, and the person following him) but tugging at me as well.

The man following Evie is, in turn, being followed. (Evie is not yet ready to let her mind clarify the fact that what is following the man is not a person but an animal, a creature.) She has with her a walkie-talkie, of sorts, a 1980s-era

General Electric, rectangular and boxy with an antenna that, when fully extended, stretches out to 3 or 4 feet. It's actually not a walkie-talkie (although that's what she and the others call them) but a C.B. transceiver, and in the old analog way, its signal manages to go undetected by the digital network. Atop the rock outcropping, Evie understands that this is a good time for a strong signal and so she unpacks the transceiver, switches it to high power, channel B, and speaks. As absurd as it makes her feel to speak it, she asks the corny question.

"Do you read me, Micah?"

She depresses the side button, waits, and then speaks again. The signal is slow. Time passes. There's a hissing noise coming from the walkie-talkie. A skinny dust devil emerges like a dangling thread and then disappears in the distance. Evie imagines the signal skipping between the desert floor and the sky. She imagines that birds can sense it as they fly through it, that it touches their little brains and sets them off course ever so slightly. She feels, as she always does, the weird thrill of depressing the button to speak, the vulnerability of releasing her words into the air.

The birds of *Beyond Blue Tomorrows*. Michelle had said, *fix the birds.*

How to describe the *descriptions* of birds in *Tomorrows*?

Its author was either familiar with the birds themselves,

or with old field guides (and I say old because some of the turns of phrase seem oddly remote from the present time) or both. They were an essential—if improbable—part of the book. Why improbable? Because the details of their lives and habits were somehow more intimate than the human characters Evie, the man following her (whose name, we learn midway through the book, is Nikolai), and the person/object following him. For instance, as Evie scrambles down the rock outcropping we learn than she comes across a loggerhead shrike nest in a bush, and that she flushes the birds by coming too close, and that *the food of the loggerhead is entirely animal in character* and that one Professor F. E. L. Beal reported in 1912 to little fanfare that the contents of 88 loggerhead stomachs showed a breakdown of 68 percent insects, four percent spiders, and 28 percent vertebrates, mostly mice.

"Micah, do you read me?" Silence, again.

She has been trained to be patient and to wait through this silence.

She unscrews the canteen and takes a swig.

In the distance, across the vast plain of sand, because of the angle of the sun, the figure following her carries a long shadow, and she notices that, in fact, the person is no longer moving toward her. He has stopped, a black pencil line in the desert, and she sees the flashes of the binoculars and knows she is being watched. And then, perhaps because the light is just right, she notices something else: that the desert floor is not uniform, but rather very lightly tracked. From her high vantage point, it looks to Evie like snail tracks, or those grooves that wood-boring insects leave beneath the bark that shags off dead branches.

The transceiver emits a shock of static. Her cue to simply depress the "push to talk" button, hold it for three seconds, and release.

She turns her attention back to the tracks. They seem random, but Evie's training is to find order and potential meaning in randomness. Her first instinct is that the tracks were made to look random. This, of course, is the sort of thing that the people who sent her on this expedition would want to hear. She also wonders if perhaps they're crude runways for the drones, or directional markings of some sort. As the sun lowers itself on the horizon behind her, the vast sky before her begins to take on that pinkish blue color, slowly deepening into a bruised purple. A slight wind has picked up, and Evie zips her canvas jacket.

Another burst of static and then the familiar voice "What have you seen?" it asks.

"The same one's following me. And then another behind him."

"How far behind?"

"A half a day. Maybe more. Neither of them are moving now."

The sky continues to ripen. There is a coolness settling over the desert.

"Anything else?"

Evie is about to mention the track marks on the desert floor. And then she decides against it.

There is a feeling in her, instinctual, that it's important that she not reveal everything, that she hold something back.

Although she tries to push it down, images of the terrible things she saw in the basement float to the surface of her mind, and she hesitates.

Will they know she's lying? "No. Nothing else," she says. There is silence.

Then a sharp hiss of static.

She knows that the conversation, such as it was, is over.

The occasional solid lines that run margin to margin were part of the manuscript as we received it and were weirdly persistent. At first we thought the lines had some bearing on the narrative itself and had been placed there intentionally. But we decided at last they were simply a distraction and tried to remove them but no matter how we modified the digital file the solid lines persisted to the point of exasperation and so *Tomorrows* was published with the lines.

Michelle's theory was that *Beyond Blue Tomorrows* was written by someone working against the protectorate, disguised as someone working for the protectorate. Evie, in Michelle's eyes, was intended as a pro-protectorate parable at the level of story: the plot and events of her journey loosely align with the goals of the protectorate. However, at a second level—the level of discourse—*Beyond Blue Tomorrows* reveals itself as a subversive text. That is, in its telling, its narration (for no story is told apart from the strategies for telling it) it's a story about undoing power. Evie, in this reading, is a hero against spectacle, determined to destroy the image of the well as much as the well itself.

The next morning, just before sunrise, Evie continues, and before the sun has been up for very long the landscape has changed. She knows there will be a ruin soon, a place she must stop at and survey. Some years ago, during her training, she read an essay that distinguished between inner syntax—how you talk to yourself—as opposed to outer syntax—how you talk to others. Evie considered this upon her horse, in this landscape that was slowly changing from arid to grasslands. "The quivering inner words"—she remembered that phrase in particular.

She wondered about the horse, Red, and what sort of thoughts it had, and if those thoughts ever conspired into language. What does a horse think

when it thinks? Does it even think? It communicates
with her; that much Evie knows. Its ears twitch
in pleasure when she comes close, and the thought
of this makes her lean forward to rub gently the
smooth, nearly hairless bridge of its snout. In the
low, dry, outcroppings of grass that begin to dot
the desert floor, little gray birds flit to and fro.

In truth, Evie had been designated to repair this
portion of the well a long time ago. She had been
recruited in college, although she didn't know it
at the time. It was her math professor, Dr. Hern,
in whose number theory class she had fallen in love
with Diophantus and the sort of pure mathematics
that was supposedly transcendent and unmoored from
the physical world. Over long discussions in his
green painted cinder-block office, a thread began
to emerge, so thin and tenuous that it would be
years before Evie would even notice it, and then
more years beyond that until she would come to
understand its meaning.

At the time, it appeared as if the talk was all
math, Dr. Hern always circling back to Pierre
de Fermat, the seventeenth- century amateur
mathematician whose "last theorem" was, according
to Hern, a political manifesto disguised as a
math riddle. These conversations, which ate up his
entire office hours, mirrored in their own way long
equations, extending out from some vague center
though thickets of parentheses and symbols that
to the untrained eye look like a secret code or a

simulation of a secret code. Evie didn't see at
the time (although she did feel it, that something
was not as it should have been) that together, she
and Hern were laying down two tracks at the same
time: one pure math, and one pure theory. But not
number theory. Rather, political theory.

For in their long, speculative, problem-solving
sessions what was really at stake was not so much
the balancing of equations as the balancing of
ideas, ideas about power and its distributive
properties, the way its elliptical curving makes
it seem natural and invisible. Only later would
Evie understand what Hern was teaching her: that
ideas are not there for the finding but only come
into focus through the act of solving, and that
number theory is an act of interpretation that,
for Dr. Hern and eventually Evie, leaked out beyond
the world of math into the world of politics and
power. College was also the first time that Evie
had ever heard anyone speak openly of the wells,
which led in turn to her uttering the word "well"
for the very first time in her life.

Her family had been Strict Constructionists: the
new laws (new at the time that Evie was in junior
high) that forbade the transmission of information
about sites of national security, which her parents
interpreted to mean: no talking about the wells, or
the military bases, or the nuclear power plants, or
the towers. In fact, Evie—like everyone else—only
learned that they were called "wells" through the

list of verboten national security sites broadcast each night on the television. And even this itself she had always found curious: that the government would bring attention to the very places it forbade people to talk about.

The phrase label "Strict Constructionist" was Michelle's idea, inserted into the text by her. I'd been against this sort of aggressive editing, preferring to delete rather than add to *Tomorrows*.

Of course, some families did talk about these places. In fact, her best friend's father would read aloud, in a mocking, false-authoritative voice, the very site names that scrolled down the television screen late at night when, during sleepovers at Laura's house, Evie would fall asleep wondering about the differences between Laura's father and her own. Was this man more brave, more heroic than her father, who would never dare to speak the word "well," let alone in a register that suggested a playful—yet undeniably defiant—tone? Or was her father the courageous one, suppressing with a tremendous and heroic act of willpower his desire to speak the forbidden words?

And the first real fight she had with Laura had been over these words, for Laura interpreted Evie's refusal to speak them— lying on top of her sleeping bag on that hot summer night on the floor of Laura's bedroom—as some sort of slight against her own father. It was such a real and visceral falling out,

the silences between them that night stretching on
and on, and Evie took such pleasure in crying and
in the perverse strength she felt in not succumbing
to Laura's demands that she speak the word "well."
But secretly, in a way that Laura would never
know, Evie had begun to doubt her father's wisdom
that night. And by the end of that summer and into
the fall her father had narrowed in her mind. She
never would have guessed that her father knew this,
that he felt the change in her, and that, in fact,
her reaction against his strict adherence to the
government's word rules was absolutely essential
in preparing her for the sort of dangerous future
she would inherit.

Michelle and I had many disputes over the final shape
and contents of *Beyond Blue Tomorrows*. She, for instance,
preferred the title *Beyond the Blue Horizon* and the way the
pentameter words galloped through the title.

The birds are gone.

And some part of Evie has left with them, to take
wing over the vast savannah and to not alight until
they have reached the well.

She has a perverse desire to turn around and ride
Red right straight for the man following her, and
to have it be done with once and for all. To break
with the script. To think thoughts and to say words
that she was never meant to say. To cut the throat
of the man following her and if need be become red,

blood-red, like her horse's name—red, Red, RED—and
then to continue backtracking to those who sent
her on this absurd mission and murder them too,
and thus in thinking such thoughts she becomes a
rebel of the mind. She has made a decision, Evie
has. She will carry out her assignment—she has no
choice; the drones make sure of that—with such
ruthless efficiency (has she been hustling them all
along?) that not only will the well be repaired
but it will be strengthened, made more powerful in
ways that will disrupt the very systems that have
sent her here in the first place.

The well is not made of stone, as they believe it
is.

Strange, Evie thinks: they have never been to the
well themselves, and yet they are certain about
its physical characteristics. But Evie is more
interested in its psychological characteristics,
slumbering now and for a long time, but ready to
awaken. For the well has polluted not just the
land, but thought, too. It took Evie a long time
to figure this out and to come to understand that
the well's purpose was not just to sicken the
citizenry into a dull form of obedience, but also
to contaminate their thoughts.

I'd like to come back to this idea of contamination, for
this is what truly haunted Michelle. She seemed genuinely
to believe that *Tomorrows* was much more than simply a
manuscript. At times, in fact, she referred to it as a *rhizome*,

something that is always being produced, that has no definable entry or exit point, that spreads in unforeseeable ways. One dark night in particular Michelle told me she feared that elements of *Tomorrows* had leaked out and spread into the world. At first I thought she meant that portions of the manuscript itself had leaked, but in fact she meant something larger, more dangerous. *Elements of the world described in the manuscript,* she had said, *have entered the world as we know it.* I countered that the manuscript already *was* of this world. *That's not what I mean,* she said, and went on to describe how before she even had heard of or received the manuscript she came across several of the physical and geological elements described in the book.

That Evie is immune to this is clear to her, and yet here, too, she is not sure why. But she has her suspicions, for as a girl, there was an accident involving the well, a "breach" that endangered the entire country. In their rush to return home and to safety, there had been, on a remote stretch of desert road, a terrible accident that killed her father and maimed her mother. Stranded in a wrecked car, unable to free herself, she languished for two days, breathing in the contaminated air, unprotected by the filters that everyone else was using—had been trained to use—in case of such an emergency. By the time she was discovered, her mother, too, was dead, and Evie had breathed in enough of the toxic air to have killed her. And yet, although she was sickened for weeks, she thrived afterwards. Evie has come to believe that the poison, rather than killing her, inoculated her.

We certainly had our arguments over this bit. That sentence about inoculation was part of a larger section that Michelle felt distracted from the force and forward momentum of the narrative, claiming that the manuscript already had a tenuous through-line as it was, and that any further digressions would only further weaken its hold on the reader's imagination. I countered that the deeper we went into Evie's mind the better, even at the risk of temporarily stalling out. In the end Michelle won that round, and the passages explaining why Evie believed in the inoculation bit were cut.

From then on she was immune to the well's workings, whatever those workings were. Her thoughts, at around age nine, a year after the accident, began to run at first parallel to, and then actively against, the dominant thought of the time. She could feel it happening, the slow bubbling up of doubt, the skepticism. She also knew—instinctively, as if she was an animal whose deep gene structures were signaling it information about how to survive—that she should never utter a word about this.

That she should play along, nodding her head in agreement with the prevailing opinions and political trends, whatever they happened to be. That's also when she began to notice patterns, patterns of thought that seemed to take hold of her countrymen in regular, even obvious, cycles.

It is right and proper to call whatever it is that follows the man who follows Evie a creature, not a person.

Not a creature in the black lagoon sense, but rather something more abstract, amorphous.

It drags, rather than carries, itself along.

It walks on two legs, true enough, but only if you imagine its legs as boney stilts, stilts with more joints in them than in human legs. It is black, and oily, and its breathing is much, much slower than seems possible.

It seems flat, dimensionless.

Transparent and yet you can see it shimmering.

Its respiration system is aided by gills and vents that, every several minutes, make a soothing, raspy noise as air is drawn in, exchanged for something purer, and then exhaled. It assumes the rough shape of a man for short periods of time, to help it remember what to be later. It is not of the sand and yet understands what it means to exist as just one grain out of millions.

Evie has studied the architectural maps of the well, as she was supposed to, and so she understands that even though it is still miles away, in the distance, she is already standing over its basin, thousands of feet beneath her, and holding not water or gas but wires, the circuitry of the State. It is this circuitry that she has been sent to re-engineer, to repair, to correct so that the delicate membrane between those who wield power and those who are powerless is kept as transparent as possible, undetected. It's not clear—not clear to anyone—how this works, only that it does. The well was there before the State, a sort of pre-history that no one can remember having not been present. It reveals itself gradually, as the State advances, so that that when the first settlers encountered it all that was apparent to them was its rocky, open-air outcroppings.

Michelle became fixated with the possibility that—like the well it described—*Beyond Blue Tomorrows* had always existed and this idea of hers was so absurd that we laughed about it. In truth, I was taken aback that Michelle would share this with me, this weird belief. I knew that's when I loved her, at that moment, and I remember she was wearing a yellow dress and pale blue tights and, for me, that's the snapshot image of Michelle I carry around in my head. The surge of love was so strong that I knew right away that even if it began fading then and there it would take years—it would take forever—for that love to diminish.

Something startling, but not impossible. A relic, they called it, from the people who must have been here first. As time passed and the State grew and exterminated the land's inhabitants and advanced in technological and other ways, more of the well was discovered, parts that matched the technologies of the time. And so it was that the vast reservoired circuitry had been discovered recently, node connecting to node with no apparent center, its loose architecture somehow corresponding to the idea of the Internet itself. And so when it was re- discovered by the protectorate it made sense; there was something to compare it to, something that suggested that it—the well—was of our time, even though, most clearly, it was not.

The tools at Evie's disposal—the tools she is to use to repair the well—are instruments so delicate that they don't yet exist. Properly speaking. Of course they do exist, but not in their tool shape, not yet. They exist now as a seeds, of a sort, that when exposed to the wiring of the well will activate, and come to life as proper tools. This allows Evie to carry what would otherwise be hundreds of pounds of metal. Now, in their pre-tool state, they look like coins. She can hear them sometimes when the horse gallops, jangling together in the worn leather satchel, and it is a comforting sound that reminds her of counting her father's loose change when he would come home from work. Still warm from his pocket, the pennies and nickels and dimes and occasional quarter seemed to her a weirder form of currency, currency charged-through with her father's thoughts and movements of the day. There are those of us concerned with this association. The association between the seed-tools and Evie's memory of her father's coins.

Together, we fell in love with this part about Evie's father and the coins. It was the only time we talked about relations, about families. This must have been not long after we discovered that Michelle was pregnant.

The man following Evie is much closer now. She can almost see his face. Upon his horse he comes slowly towards her. All the threat, the dread, has drained away. Somehow Evie understands that whatever the man's intentions, she shall not be harmed. Not by him. He is close now. Closer. Red snorts, his ears twitching. Evie rubs his flank and murmurs something soothing in his ear. The man dismounts. He is caked in dust and Evie practically laughs at this, the absurd particularness of his dirtiness, so dirty that it makes her wonder about her own state of cleanliness.

He smiles.

A genuine smile.

He is tall and wears a strap of large, brassy bullets across his chest, like costuming out of an old Western. There is something wrong with his face, something hard to define at first but that gradually reveals itself: a scar that cuts so deeply across his chin it's as if part of it is missing. There is a kindness to the way he stands there, beside his horse, and when a cloud passes overhead casting him in shadow Evie notices other details: the red bandana tied around the ankle part of his left boot; the unlit cigarette that's between the fingers of one hand; the dark red epaulette affixed to the

shoulder part of his right sleeve. The first thing
he does is to bring his horse over to Red, who takes
no offense at this other horse. He then produces a
spotted apple, holding it first for Red, and then
for his own horse. In this way, the horses share
a meal, and there is no animosity between them.

Michelle had initially believed that the real story being
told here remained hidden between the words and lines.
This—this hidden story—was the one that Michelle wanted
to rescue from *Tomorrows*. In order to do that, she needed
someone (me) to track down the obscure source material
that lay fallow between the lines and to resurrect it, as it
were, transforming *Tomorrows* into the second story obscured inside. In a way, it's like tracing dirty money back to
its source, and maybe that's why Michelle sought me out,
for my training in this art of exposing concealment which,
although it's the opposite of what I did in the financial networks (where my job was to conceal, not reveal, money)
perhaps Michelle understood that in order to expose, one
needed to know, first, how to conceal. But how do you find
feeling in a text where there is none? How far does the reader
have to dig until what's being revealed has nothing to do with
the text at hand and everything to do with the reader's own
subjective needs projected onto the text?

Around sunset, talk turns to the well. His name, he
says (and Evie has no reason not to believe him)
is Steadman. He has been sent in service of the
well, as support to Evie.

"You believe that?" she asks.

"What?"

"That you were sent to back me up?"

The fire licks and snaps like small yellow flags in the dark.

"I believe that I've been sent to do more than that."

"Than what?"

"Back you up."

They are sitting across from each other, the fire between them, the horses in the background, sleeping or just still. The air is clear and cool. The blue-black sky is full of stars.

Steadman reminds Evie of someone, someone from a long time ago, before she began working as an engineer for the State.

"So we're just going to talk openly about it," he says. Evie pauses, considers the meaning behind his words. "Does it matter if we talk openly or secretly? Either way we're not saying anything wrong. Just talking about the mission."

"You don't think doubting is wrong?"

"Just asking if you think the only reason you were sent was to back me up. That's not doubt."

A coyote yips in the distance, and then is joined by another, and then there is a chorus, their high voices carrying far across the open desert.

"Think they're real?" Steadman asks. Evie lets the question slot into her head. "You ever read that Bradbury story? About the kids' room that's a virtual veldt in Africa except the lions are real and they eat the parents, maybe?"

"Like the holodeck," Evie says.

"The thing about the holodeck is: I always thought inside the holodeck was the 'real' space, and it was the outside that was simulated."

Steadman pauses. Lets it sink in.

"And ever notice," he says, "how what happens in the holodeck sometimes leaks out? In one episode, Picard is kissed by a woman and comes out with lipstick on his cheek."

The coyotes are closer now, and Evie takes a revolver—a bright red revolver—from inside her boot, and sets it on the wool blanket on her lap.

"The thing is, and it's pretty obvious, is that when you're watching a show like that, there's no real difference between 'virtual' reality and reality itself. They're both there embodied on the screen."

"'Embodied.' You sound like the theorists who sent us."

In the distance, behind Steadman, Evie notices a light flashing, a pin-prick of light that must be coming from the mountain range dozens of miles away. She waits to see if it's a pattern.

"I guess it's true. I learned to talk like them. In training. Didn't you?"

"I can't tell anymore. Do you think I talk like them?"

"I haven't heard you talk enough to say."

By now it's clear that the flashing light is intentional, and Evie motions to Steadman. He watches it in silence and when he looks back at Evie she's jotting something in a small blue notebook. It's basic Morse:

. . . - —— . —.

STOP

Have I mentioned that parts of *Tomorrows*—the version of the report that I have—had been redacted and then un-re-dacted? This was a big source of dispute between Michelle and I early on. Her claim was always that this, the report I was given to work with, was the closest to the original that could be secured, a claim which I did eventually come to believe. But early on I was skeptical, for it seemed to me there *was* an earlier version, perhaps many earlier versions, that hadn't been redacted.

You don't redact something as you're writing it. For the report to mean anything, it had to be whole. That was my thinking at the beginning, my purist thinking. For I, too, had been trained by the protectorate. A different sort of training than Evie or Steadman underwent, of course, and yet we were all working toward the same goal: the repair of the well that would result in an accurate documentation of that repair. The report came to me in the old analog way: in a black binder. It had been printed on graphing paper, which made things both easier and more difficult to read. Mostly more difficult. There were many protocols that I was required to follow the first time, protocols that struck me as absurd and ritualistic. I was, for instance, permitted to read *Tomorrows* in a secure room and instructed not to open the folder until the red light at the corner of the desk lit up. And I was to keep my hands atop the desk during the duration of my reading. After several visits, none of these requirements were enforced, and eventually I was permitted to take the report with me when I left.

An addendum to the report contains fragments of information about the creature. The first fragment concerns itself with whether *creature* is even the right word. Others are suggested, tried out. Eventually *creature* is decided upon. Other fragments in the addendum ("the creature part," as I came to think of it) offer speculative details about its size and shape but these are heavily redacted, so all that's left are some terms that appear oddly stark on the page, surrounded as they are by thick black redactions. The creature's unstable, unmappable state is reflected in the way it's described in weird, contradictory terms. Sometimes the creature is simply a geometric shape hovering just above the desert floor. Other times it's more akin to an oil spill in the air, spreading black against a blue sky.

The so-called stilts come and go: they appear only when the creature is really on the move. And yet, despite all the textual roadblocks and turn-arounds there are passages that really affected me, and that I fought hard to preserve in my summary account, and that spoke to the strange, dependent relationship that Evie, Steadman, and the creature developed, for without Evie there would be no need for Steadman, and without Evie and Steadman, there would be no creature, all of them gravitating towards the well, the widening spell of the well. I took the parts featuring the creature very seriously—*too* seriously, according to Michelle, in an assessment that turned out to be right—and tried, for a time, to impose the loose, chaotic structure of the creature onto the manuscript itself.

STOP.

"Of course, that means GO," Evie says to Steadman. This was her way of deflecting one truth off another, of protecting her true and pure thoughts, which at that point were as scrambled as Steadman's when it came to the meaning, let alone the source, of the Morse-flashing light. In truth, the flashing light terrified her. She hadn't expected to have been watched by anyone other than Steadman and the creature, and the light meant either that she had been wrong or that there was someone, something, beyond the power of the State watching her. Was STOP a warning or a taunt? Worse yet, was it a signal from the well itself, its first act of self-protection? It was at this point—the fading campfire between them—that Evie considered the uses that might be made of Steadman.

The shakiness of Beyond Blue Tomorrows. The pressures of giving it shape. How not to become infected by the same creeping thought that infected the others, those who were NOT selected to repair the well. This was always the problem. We all knew that, no matter what iteration, the Tomorrows report was compromised in some way, having been written in such close physical proximity to the well, and I think that's why I was confined to a room for the first reading. It's true that the report blurred in and out of focus, always at the same pages, and that some of them gave off just a hint of low-reverb sound. The first time Michelle kissed me was with the report in her hand, with my fingers touching it, too.

The well is in the distance, but also underfoot. As they make their way out of the brief respite of the savannah and back into the flat desert, this becomes more clear than any theory.

Evie and Steadman, each on horses with their own horse-thoughts unrecorded, understand in separate but connected ways that the flashing light signals mean that they must keep moving. The fire damped out. Evie's red gun tucked severely away. The day growing hot enough to blank out and erase all bad, dissident thought.

The desert opening an impossible passage before them, one only the horses can detect. They ride in silence, the eerie silence of early morning, before the heat, the horses sure of their steps in the hard, salty sand. The flashing signal now like a third presence, a third person even, disembodied as a blinking eye but alive, alive and watching, seeking. The horses even aware somehow, their ears more nervous than before.

Was Evie supposed to see Steadman's weapon? A silver, insect-like thing attached to his belt, revealed briefly as he shifts in his saddle. The noon sun glints off it and it catches her eye, but not while he's looking. He hasn't seen that she's seen, has he?

The bandits approach from the east. On low, fast horses. The afternoon angle of the sharp sun had obscured them. By the time they came into vision it was too late to do anything but face them. A woman and a man, their faces scarred and dark and tight from the sun. They circle Evie and Steadman, their horses leaner than theirs.

"We saw you. We been seeing you," the woman says. "We been seeing you for days we have." There's something about her voice, the cadence of her words, not an accent but a weird lilt, as if she learned, unlearned, and then re-learned English. Two responses come into Evie's brain, and she chooses this one: "We've been watching you watch us."

The woman draws her horse away and then comes back, this time to Steadman. Evie notices a brand on its flank, something like an upside down triangle. "Can we help you get where you're going?" she asks Steadman, although it was more of a statement than a question. She holds Steadman's eyes and then the man comes closer too and says, "He don't know where he's goin' without her," nodding to Evie.

"They dragged that territory with them behind," the woman says.

"You seen it as good as I," the man replies. His horse snorts and he rubs its spotted head.

"Got to cut that territory loose," she says.

"Cut it free from the bone," he replies.

The woman suddenly—how did Evie miss this?—has something like a tomahawk in her hand, its head misshapen as if it had been partially melted in a fire. She holds it to her side. It's not a threat, except that it is. She leans forward on her horse and holds it before its nose, as if asking it to smell it. Then she reaches over and hands it to the man, who tucks it into a leather satchel. Next he opens another satchel and removes another, different tomahawk, this one slightly larger and even more unshaped or unbalanced than the first one.

He hands the tomahawk or whatever back to the woman and she does something like spit on it although it's not as crude as that, as spitting.

Steadman slides his hand down to his weapon that only Evie knows about and the woman raises the tomahawk as if posing for a picture that was historical except that it was not historical blood that would be spilled. There is movement in the sand like something from distorted VHS and the horses sense it first, all four shifting at roughly the same time to face a new direction, compass-like, obeying as if this had somehow been pre-programmed into their horse brains. The weapon, Steadman's weapon, grows and breathes like an animated lung and the tomahawk, too, seems to quiver with potential. Steadman doesn't hold his weapon threateningly, just as if. He puts it across his lap.

The woman waves her tomahawk like a wand but nothing happens. Maybe nothing is supposed to happen. "Four people two weapons," the man says, as if thinking aloud, "plus those territories," as if they were people too.

"Get that thing brother," the woman says to the man, referring, it seems, to Steadman's weapon and it occurs to Evie just then that they might be, in fact, brother and sister. Their movements mirror each other, in a strange way that suggests a deeper symmetry.

"Give it here," the man says, holding out his hand to Steadman, as if Steadman would just give it over. Steadman raises the weapon, which seems to vibrate and gently expand and contract like a living thing. What would have happened next is interrupted by a distant howl, low and full, its sound speeding across the desert. The oily creature, the one that moves as if on stilts. Although it's not visible, Evie and Steadman feel its presence, somewhere in the distance, warning them with its mournful call. The brother and sister feel it too, and the stand-off is diffused. Steadman puts his weapon away, and so does the sister.

"You go on your way," she says to Evie, "but cut those territories loose before you get there."

"Get where?" says Evie.

"To what you call the well. Buried in our country. That thing coming will stop you so we won't have to."

"Your country?"

"That well is ours. We done things to it."

"What things?" Evie asks.

"You'll see."

Unoccupied by the bandits the space around them seems different now. Evie feels highlighted, as if the presence of the bandits had somehow marked her, made her hyper-visible and maybe Steadman feels this too for he's the one to say "we better move." They ride faster than they have before, their horses hoofing across the sand, their ears back and flat against their heads and the freedom Evie feels moving fast and hard astride the muscle that is her horse is unlike anything she has felt for a long time. The desert seems to change color, slowly, from dull yellow to bright yellow the faster she goes, Steadman on his horse parallel to hers, the light continuing to evolve and the taste of sand in Evie's mouth changing too, from something bitter to something almost sweet.

The shadow of something very large planes across the desert in front of them, disappearing into the distance. In the blue sky, Evie sees something black and distant. Then the shadow turns and comes back, this time sweeping over them. The air seems to cool momentarily, and Evie understands how exposed they are. They slow their horses to a trot and Steadman says, "You think it's one of them?"

"If it is there'll be others."

Drones with feathers, as if anyone would think they were actually birds, giant birds whose wings didn't flap. And yet it was someone's idea to do this, part of a larger trend that saw technology take on the aura of the natural world.

The mouth in the sand is not a mouth in the sand. But it is close.

100 yards. Or so.

That is a safe distance to watch as the desert disappears into a hole in itself, a spinning hole of sand like something in the ocean, like something in a children's book. Or the sort of thought that gives rise to a children's book whose pages are deserts of thought, on-and-on and blank and blank in expanses of soft brown and tan, divided with a horizontal razor-line of blue sky. There is no accumulated thought in a place where nothing grows that counts. The heretical human-ness of the cactus.

At some point it was decided—by whom? by what?—that the report needed an incident. *If the report is to succeed, an incident must occur both in the story proper as well as in the framing narrative that constitutes the conditions of its telling.* Michelle was the one who told me about this, early one morning after the first night that I had spent at her place, an apartment on the edge of the city, a morning of such strong light that it seemed as if the day had already accumulated itself into one moment.

"The framing narrative?" I asked.

"I know, right? Me too!" she said. I took this to mean that she was as bewildered by that part of the instruction as I was. Michelle told me that these marching orders (that's what she called them) had been delivered over night via the e-mail account of someone at the agency who was a reliable source of information about its intentions. The agency's, that was. It so happened that this way of talking about the agency had crept into Michelle's vocabulary so that the agency took on a gender (*she*) and, pardon the pun, a sort of agency of its own, as in, *I guess that's what she wants*, or, *I'll have to ask the agency*.

"Does that mean us?" I asked her. "Does what?"

"That we're the framing narrative? The ones telling the story about the well, about

Beyond Blue Tomorrows?"

A look of panic or confusion swept over Michelle's face. It must have been contagious, because for a moment I too was overcome with a feeling of helplessness, a kind of vertigo even, and I felt that awful tingling in my stomach, like when an elevator descends too quickly. I think it was the sudden clarity that caused it, the putting into one phrase—*we're the framing narrative*—of a thought that up to that point had remained vague and unspoken and not fully formed. This wasn't some meta-fictional conundrum about how story-tellers inevitably make themselves the subject of the stories they tell no matter how hard they try to hide themselves or disappear, in the "death of the author" sense. Nor was it some literary rehash of the so- called quantum observer effect whereby the act of observing an object somehow changes it.

But of course we'd already framed the narrative—we just didn't know it yet. Because I can't end without saying something *else* about the night Michelle and I spent together at her place. It would be too weirdly metaphysical to say that we wanted to create something that night, something that would outlast *Beyond Blue Tomorrows*, something infinitely more complex than the story told by Evie's journey, something there in that room with the blue moonlight coming in amid half-unpacked boxes of books awaiting half-put-together bookshelves. The trees outside her apartment bent in the wind and cast the room in a kind of swirling, reverse mirror ball light, her long naked body on the bed, the two of us sharing each other before we went our separate ways and became other, more dangerous people.

Antony's Story

WHAT THEY DID TO ME WAS EVERYTHING BUT KILL ME. THEY destroyed me, but they didn't kill me.

They left enough of me.

Enough of what's inside of me. They shoved letters in my face they said were from my sister. From my Rachel. I couldn't read them.

I didn't read them.

I can't read in the dark. They left enough of me. Rachel.

They left something inside me. Something enough to rebuild myself. To rebuild parts of myself.

I'm grateful.

It went dark and a bag was shoved over my head. It stank of ammonia.

I was in the church and it went dark. Rachel's letters.

They left enough of me.

Something was shoved into my ribs. Please I screamed please.

I couldn't breathe.

I am so grateful.

It went dark again and then I don't remember and then I was lying on a mattress somewhere. I was so thirsty. It was dark. I heard a door open and a gust of air moved the bag on my head. Please, I tried to say, please, but my throat was so dry. So grateful.

Someone yanked off the bag. The door opened and shut again. It was still dark. I tried to swallow.

I could stand. I could walk.

I touched the room with my fingers. Concrete walls, concrete floor.

They said the walls were papered with letters from my sister. On my hands and knees I touched.

A drain.

I heard an animal in the drain. A crack in the wall.

The frame of a door. There were noises. There was laughter.

My sister's letters laughed. Rachel.

I stood on the bed and tried to touch the ceiling. I tried to catch the laughter.

The door opened and light came in.

It hurt my eyes. It's okay, said a voice. A man's voice. It's okay. What's your name? I tried to speak but it hurt so much. It was just air. I tried to say water. The light went off and the bag was pushed over my head. I tried to scream. There were noises. I heard laughter.

In my mind my thirst became an object. A pebble.

A pebble lodged in my throat. If I could only swallow it.

That would be better than drinking. There is no metal in me.

Paul Paul a long way to fall. The taller the faller.

The giant with metal parts. There is no metal in me.

Dear Antony.

Dear Antony I hope.

Dear Antony I hope you are receiving. Dear Antony are you receiving?

Later, the door opened. I heard it open. I felt the air. But there were no footsteps. No sounds. Not even the sound of laughter. Later the door. I heard it open. There is no metal.

They did not take all of me. They left a part of me.

For my sister.

Dear brother.

Dear Antony are you receiving?

Dear brother the girls are crying for their father. Later show me how.

Let me take your hand. Let us walk through sand. My brain burned.

Later the door opened.

The ring in the sand opened. The well opened.

The well opened and closed. Dear Antony.

Dear sister.

The sound of laughter was like water, and they took that away. A pebble in my throat.

What they did to me. What they did to me was. There is no metal in me. Paul Paul.

They took me across the sand.

I tried to imagine that the dark was water, and that I was swimming in the water. I crawled across the floor to the drain. I laid on my stomach and I was floating. I stretched my arms out to swim. I floated above the floor. The water was cold. The current worked against me. I pulled myself forward through the water with my arms. I turned my head to breathe, then turned and held my breath, then turned my head to breathe. There were layers of water and I was on the top layer. A light opened far beneath me and I could see the drain. The drain was green. I was in the cell the drain. The room was filled with water. I was on top of the water. I was free. I was naked.

The black metal pole that disappeared. That disappeared into the ceiling. It went on and on. Up and up.

Oh Antony.

Are you receiving?

The green drain was my guide. I wanted to laugh.

I wanted to shout with joy.

And then the green light stopped. The drain was clouded.

The water became harder.

The pebble of thirst came back. A red pebble.

A red marble.

I could feel the bottom of the water.

I palmed the puddles on the cement floor. I grabbed the pole and my fingers sunk in.

The door opened, with light. A boot shoved me from the drain. I gasped for air. There were layers of water. I was drowning. I was drowning on air. I was heaved and hurled to the bed. Someone pulled off my hood. I kicked at the air. Someone grabbed my foot and twisted it. I tried to yell out. The pain jumped from my ankle to my brain. My brain burned. Emberhead. I was shaking my head to put out the fire. A hand grabbed my throat and shouted STOP! I breathed. I tried to breathe. The fire in my head smoked out. I was panting. I was gasping. Emberhead. They took a part of me. They left part of me. They were kind. There is the drain. There is the door. Dear Antony. Dear Antony please. Dear Antony are you. The door opened with light. The light opened the door and came in.

We could play one note for you, a voice said. One note that would last all your life. Someone took me by the wrist and said Open Your Hand. A cold water bottle.

The shape of a drain.

The shape of The One Who Comes in the Night. A drain for thoughts.

I drank and drank and dislodged the pebble from my throat. Someone yanked the bottle away.

I'm grateful.

It moved along the wall.

You could drink like that forever. We could play that note forever. Does she carry a banner?

They left enough of me.

Emberhead.

The door shut, and it was dark. It moved it crawled.

We could play one note for you. We could play that note forever.

In the dark I traced the shape of myself, I tried to remember my body. I started with my toes and moved up, tracing the outline.

There was the sound of something in the cell. Something in the cell. Something else.

It moved it crawled.

I heard it breathing, its rattling breathing. What had they left in the room with me? I tried to be so still to listen.

Sometimes the breathing stopped.

Was it listening to me? It was so dark. The breathing was coming from the back of the cell, from behind me, from opposite where the door was. I could see the thin thread of light around the door. Did a shape pass in front of it? Was the thing pacing the perimeter of the cell? I tried to remember day or night. The thing could be my friend. No! The thing was watching me. It could see in the dark! It could be the dark.

It wore sand. It carried sand.

Why else would it be here?

The final shape of The One Who Comes.

The final shape of The One.

It was no friend. I tried to remember my body. They did not take all of me. I tried to swim. I left the bed to swim. I crawled back to the drain. Drain can you hear me I said. Drain open up and let the water in. Drain. What had they left in the room with me? Why did it block the drain?

Dear Antony. Dear sister.

I tried to remember my body. Something was watching me. Drain can you hear me. That note, forever.

We could play that.

The man with the machine came. His face had scars. The machine was on a cart. It had wires.

Our aim is not to kill you, but to deform you, he said. Can you help us? I tried to answer but he stopped me.

What they did to me was take.

That helps, right there, he said. Right there, see? That helps. It's hard to deform yourself, but it would be easier, he said.

I tried to answer but he shoved something into my ribs and I saw white. White pain I saw white pain.

Later: show me how you would deform yourself, he said. Later show me how.

What they did to me.

I tried again to answer but he pointed to the machine. The machine, he said, can do this if you'd rather. Show me how you would deform yourself.

I pointed to myself.

I'm grateful. They left enough of me. Was someone coming for me?

The One Who Comes Comes for Me.

He smiled and walked backwards pulling the machine behind him. As the door shut I glanced behind me.

I glimpsed the thing. The One.

The breathing thing.

A stain on the cement wall. The One disguised as a stain. Long snout.

Enormous shoulders like clouds.

Long thin legs more than two like stilts. Not Charlotte but Charlotte.

The One strobed itself into my eyes. I pointed to myself. I wanted the drain back.

I wanted to swim. Show me. I pointed to myself. Show me. Show me how. I pointed to myself. The machine can do this if you'd rather. I wanted the drain back. A stain on the cement wall. Moving. Letting me watch it move.

I'm grateful.

As the door shut. As the door. It breathed again. It moved along the wall. I could feel it moving. Following following but unable to come close. I could not hear it with the bag over my head. I could not hear it through the smell. They didn't want me to hear it then.

I felt my way back to the cot. I tried to curl into myself. There was a storm outside or thunder or explosions. Were they coming for me? Was someone coming for me, fighting her way through the lines of defense? They did not take all of me. I tried to curl into myself. Oh drain. Is someone coming to rescue me?

Is someone coming to save me? Rachel Rachel.

Is she setting the fields on fire? Does she carry a banner? Is she well armed?

Is she coming across the fields on a horse? Has she shaken off the sand?

Does she wear her bandoliers like sashes over her shoulders? Do they contain many bullets?

The storm passed. The breathing closer. Had The One escaped the wall? Had it escaped its dimension? Was it free of time and space?

Is Rachel coming? Send Rachel.

Send Rachel coming.

The door was open I went to it. There were men in the hall, at a table. It smelled like a gym. The men were playing cards. They were laughing. I walked past them to a larger door.

I walked through that door and then through another larger door still. I felt something in my pocket and I knew what it was.

The red marble. All my hope.

All my hope.

Dear sister. Dear sister. Dear sister I remember. Dear sister I remember you. Dear sister you are like me. Dear sister bring the girls.

I remember now.

The texture of the marble taking me back.

I could feel its color. I'd learned how to feel color. To feel. I stepped out, and into the new day.

Acknowledgements

MY DEEPEST GRATITUDE TO CHRISTOPH AND LEZA FOR believing in this book and to Joel Amat Güell for the amazing cover and to Kaitlyn Kessinger and the whole CLASH gang. I'm thankful to Tina Pohlman for suggestions about the novel's structure that helped me solve a problem I was having with chronology. I am indebted to Pamela Constable and Arturo Velenzuela's *A Nation of Enemies: Chile Under Pinochet*, Robert O. Paxton's *The Anatomy of Fascism*, Thomas J. Sugrue's *The Origins of the Urban Crisis: Race and Inequality in Postwar Detroit*, and Ellen Willis's *Beginning to See the Light*. *Beyond Blue Tomorrows* is nicked from *On High in Blue Tomorrows*, from *Inland Empire*.

For Niko, Maddy, and Chandler.

For Lisa.

NICHOLAS ROMBES is author of the novel *The Absolution of Roberto Acestes Laing* as well as the 33 1/3 book *Ramones* and the experimental film book *10/40/70*. He teaches at the University of Detroit Mercy, in northwest Detroit.

A Note from the Author-Function

I hope you enjoyed the show. If you're sorry to see it end, don't worry, it ain't over 'til it's over, as they say, and it ain't over, or at least it doesn't have to be. Needless to say, I have special access to the characters you've just read about (with the exception of Chu Chu), a few of whom still exist, as it turns out, although in deep hiding. You've perhaps heard the old saw about "characters coming to life on the page?" Well, for Patti from Psycho Femmes (you remember her?) it's literally true: without your reading eyes, she's all but dead. That's right: you, dear reader, are the only thing keeping Patti tenebrously alive. Pretty heavy! But like I said, no worries.

By special arrangement with the implied author of this novel (never heard of Wayne C. Booth before?—well look him up!) I'm still in contact with Patti, and she's desperate to stay "read," which is to say, "alive." Simply snail-mail me the simple form, below, and you will receive, via return post:

- A thank you note from Patti, as well as several frames from a 16mm film of the band in concert never before released

- A personalized audio file thank you from Patti herself, sent to you via your email, Instagram, or your preferred receivership.

——————cut here, along the dotted line——————

Your name:

Your mailing address:

Your e-mail (optional):

MAIL THIS TO:
Nick Rombes
English Department, Briggs Building
University of Detroit Mercy
4001 W. McNichols Road
Detroit, MI 48221-3038

Also by CLASH Books

HOW TO GET ALONG WITHOUT ME
Kate Axelrod

GIRL LIKE A BOMB
Autumn Christian

THE RACHEL CONDITION
Nicholas Rombles

AFTERWORD
Nina Schuyler

EARTH ANGEL
Madeline Cash

ALL THINGS EDIBLE, RANDOM & ODD
Sheila Squillante

THE BLACK TREE ATOP THE HILL
Karla Yvette

PROXIMITY
Sam Heaps

VIOLENT FACULTIES
Charlene Elsby

CL<SH

WE PUT THE LIT IN LITERARY

clashbooks.com

FOLLOW US

TWITTER

IG

FB

@clashbooks

EMAIL

clashmediabooks@gmail.com

Printed in the USA
CPSIA information can be obtained
at www.ICGtesting.com
JSHW021229030424
60434JS00003B/17